I CAN FIX ANYTHING

GARY WHITEHEAD

ARSENAL PULP PRESS
Vancouver, Canada

I CAN FIX ANYTHING
Copyright © 1994 by Gary Whitehead

All rights reserved. No part of this book may be reproduced in any part by any means without the written permission of the publisher, except by a reviewer, who may use brief excerpts in a review.

ARSENAL PULP PRESS
100-1062 Homer Street
Vancouver, B.C.
Canada V6B 2W9

The publisher gratefully acknowledges the assistance of the Canada Council and the Cultural Services Branch, B.C. Ministry of Tourism and Ministry Responsible for Culture.

"I Can Fix Anything" received an Honorable Mention in the 1987 *Prism international* Short Fiction Contest. "I Love Raisins" appeared in *Dandelion* Vol. 11, No. 2 (1984). "King Kong" appeared in *Canadian Fiction* #46 (1984). "My Finite Chevy" appeared in *Zest* (1983). "She Makes the World Flat" appeared in *Writing* #12 (Summer 1985). "A Situation Comedy, Now" appeared in *Canadian Fiction* 50/51(1985) and in *Moving Off the Map: An Anthology of Contemporary Fiction* (Black Moss, 1986). "Supply and Demand" appeared in *Canadian Fiction* #71 (1991).

Typeset by the Vancouver Desktop Publishing Centre
Printed and bound in Canada by Kromar Printing

CANADIAN CATALOGUING IN PUBLICATION DATA:
Whitehead, Gary, 1957-
I can fix anything
ISBN 1-55152-001-X
I. Title.
PS8595.H5712 1994   C813'.54   C94-910271-7
PR9199.3.W5412 1994

CONTENTS

I CAN FIX ANYTHING/7

KING KONG/25

SHE MAKES THE WORLD FLAT/49

MY FINITE CHEVY/60

A SITUATION COMEDY, NOW/65

AT THE TURN OF THE CENTURY/86

I LOVE RAISINS/95

SUPPLY AND DEMAND/103

NAKED US/122

EVERYTHING IS BAMBOO/137

I CAN FIX ANYTHING

THE EMERSONS ARE PRIVATE people and very good tenants. I have met Phil several times, but I've only spoken to Connie over the phone. On the first of this month Connie arrives home early from work. Outside, it's dark and rainy.

Their apartment is in an old three-storey low-rise on the other side of town from where were we live, my mother and I.

Phil is in his study down the hall when he hears the apartment door open then slam shut. Phil's typewriter has stalled while preparing a resumé for a government job.

Connie drops the afternoon newspaper to the living room floor. Her hair is wet and she's cold. She removes her boots and kicks them into the open closet. She takes off her raincoat

I CAN FIX ANYTHING

and hangs it on a hanger, then walks slowly down the hall towards Phil's study. Her arms folded, as if in a hug, she rubs her biceps with her hands and creates a little friction. Drops of rainwater fall from her bangs and run down her cheeks. When she opens Phil's door and steps into the room, he is staring down at the stationary print unit, shaking his head from side to side.

Phil looks over his shoulder and sees Connie hugging herself. She steps back into the doorway and leans against the frame.

"Everything okay with you?" he asks, but before she can respond, he says, "Everything is *great* with me." He nods toward the machine on his desk.

"I need a shower," says Connie. "A real hot one." She turns toward the hall.

"How was work?" he says, moving in his chair, but Connie has left her place in the doorway.

Phil turns off his typewriter and follows Connie into their bathroom, next to his study. They undress and Connie steps into the shower. She begins adjusting the faucets while Phil folds and piles the clothes in two neat stacks and places them on the floor beneath the chrome towel rack. He draws the plastic shower curtain.

"You're home early," he says, stepping into the tub. "That's hot."

Since the plumbing is as old as the building, the pipes are slow to drain, and before long Connie stands in an inch of hot water in the low end of the tub. Phil lingers in the high end for a moment, then begins washing his feet.

The most striking difference between himself and Connie, aside from the obvious, is their feet. Connie's are long and slender, and her toes are dexterous in the tradition of fingers. She can control the hot and cold water faucets, change channels while watching TV, and pick fallen dice from the floor, all without lifting a hand. She stands under the hot force of the water, while Phil sits on the wide corner of the tub and wedges a well-used bar of Ivory soap between the two largest toes of his left foot.

"I hate webbed toes," says Connie, and begins shampooing. Her face is as close to the shower-head as possible unless she were to stand on her toes, and that might prove dangerous.

Phil builds up a lather in his hands and sets the soap in its dish. He is concerned with his feet for a moment, then he looks up at Connie. Shampoo suds run in waves and streams down her shiny body, around her breasts and over her stomach.

"They're not webbed, exactly," he says, smiling. "They're comfortable. They've grown close over the years." He stares down at his feet, trying to rinse them in the water that gets past Connie. "What's the matter with you?" he asks.

"I don't know how I live with a man whose toes are webbed." She turns her back to Phil, allowing the water to shower over her head and run down her face. "But that's not it."

Phil waits his turn. Despite the temperature and rising steam, a chill runs through his body and tiny goose-pimples appear on his forearms and thighs. He folds his arms across his chest, waiting.

Connie's feet have disappeared beneath the suds and rising water level in the tub. "I'm nearly done," she says, the water beating against her forehead.

"What is it then?" says Phil, and in a reflex move, raises his left eyebrow.

Connie moves from beneath the stream of water, slips by her husband, and reaches for the large, orange beach towel hanging from the chrome rack across from the toilet.

Phil closes both eyes and gropes for the bottle of shampoo on the bathroom window sill, as Connie steps from the tub and begins drying herself.

"I was fired today," she says. "Given my walking papers just like that."

Behind the plastic curtain Phil's ears fill with shampoo suds and the sound of running water. He covers his face, protecting his eyes while rinsing his hair. In a loud voice he asks, "Did someone complain? A customer?"

Connie sits on the toilet seat and dries her feet, between each delicate toe. "I love telephone sales," she says. "It makes me feel independent."

Phil turns off the water and opens the curtain. Connie is roughly drying her hair.

"I know you do," he says, but he's distracted by the water leaking from the bathtub faucet. "And you were good at it, too." He reaches for the smaller, blue towel. Their bathroom is tiny and less crowded if Phil dries himself in the tub.

"Dimitri, for one, is very satisfied with his encyclopedias." Phil glances at the dripping faucet. He begins drying his face and hair, then works his way down, saving his feet for last. "I'll nail this job tomorrow. Maybe. We'll be okay."

"Dimitri?" says Connie. She bunches the towel on her lap and looks up at the ceiling. There's a shallow depression in the plaster the shape of Ireland, next to the overhead light. "Dimitri, our landlord?"

"I called him last week." Phil lowers the blue towel from his shoulders to his back, and nods toward the faucet. "To tell him about our leak, and he mentioned that he believed you were a 'gifted telephone solicitor.'"

Connie shakes her head, drying her fine hair. "Dimitri, our landlord," she repeats, as she hangs the wet towel on the rack. "That funny little man on the phone. I remember him," she says.

Phil hikes his left foot to the rim of the tub and begins drying his thighs. "That's what he said," says Phil. "*Gifted.*"

Connie takes her matching orange bathrobe from the hook on the door. Phil bunches the towel in his hands and begins to dry his shins and calves. He looks away from what he's doing for a moment to watch Connie slip into her terrycloth robe. She draws it together in front, and ties the belt with a loose knot. She turns to face the foggy mirror above the sink and runs her hands round the back of her neck, flipping her hair from beneath the orange collar. "The whole world's crumbling around me," she says.

Phil spreads the blue towel on the floor in front of the

toilet, then pauses a moment with one foot on the rim of the tub. "That's a bit much, isn't it? The *whole* world?" He leans forward, one hand resting on his knee. "Maybe just a small piece of it?" He steps from the tub onto the towel.

"Then why am I staring at this stupid mirror?" She turns, opens the door and walks out of the tiny room.

Phil pauses a moment standing on the towel, listening to Connie's bare feet against the hardwood floor in the hall, on her way to the living room to read her afternoon paper.

Alone in the bathroom, Phil looks again to the leaking faucet. With his right hand supporting him on the wide rim of the tub, he leans over and tightens both taps with all his might, but it does no good. The water continues to drip onto the silver ring of the bathtub drain. He closes the toilet seat and settles down to dry his feet.

The afternoon shower with his wife has worked for Phil; he's revitalized, and prepared to set straight any setback. He finishes drying his feet, ignoring the dripping faucet. He dresses quickly and re-enters his study next to the bathroom.

Phil is an optimist (as Connie has informed me and as I have since seen) who refuses to believe that anything breaks, or ends, or is no longer, though he has admitted that things can change. He refers to his typewriter as *stalled*, not *broken*, as he digs through his desk drawer, locating the Olympia Owner's Manual. He resumes staring at the stationary print unit of his electronic typewriter. The steady patter from the bathtub faucet echoes down the hall.

I CAN FIX ANYTHING

Connie has a unique and gifted approach to the afternoon newspaper each day. She unfolds it on the floor, then lays down on the couch. She places an ashtray to the right of the newspaper and lights a cigarette. She leans off the couch at an awkward angle, her head hovering over the pages, her legs bent at the knees, crossed at the ankles, and her bare feet resting atop the headrest cushion. She begins with the front page and reads through until page five. This section contains the most sensational news, which is the news that most closely resembles that of the *National Enquirer*: the only paper she can enjoy start to finish because it amuses rather than annoys her. She scans the comics then turns to the Entertainment Section where she settles into the movie ads. Summer is over but there are still a lot of B-movies playing in their neighbourhood.

Phil enters the living room after he has gotten nowhere with his typewriter, and sits in the armchair next to the telephone table. He picks up the receiver and dials three fives in a row.

Connie takes the felt pen from atop the stereo. "I feel like a movie tonight," she says, and frees the plastic cap from the pen. She begins stroking black x's through movie titles.

Phil dials a six, another five, and two eights. "I'm calling Dimitri," he says.

Connie looks up from her newspaper.

✺

Both Connie and Phil enjoy renting from a landlord as

I CAN FIX ANYTHING

amiable as is theirs, all modesty aside. Although I am sometimes slow to react when repairs to the building are needed, I keep the rent well below the average for a two-bedroom apartment in their part of town; I don't come around very often except to collect the rent, and more times than not, it's very late in the month before I do even that. I deduct the yearly interest from their damage deposit plus fifty dollars from every December rent payment, which doesn't amount to a great sum, but is a civil gesture around that time of year, and I like to believe my tenants respect me for it.

❂

A little past four o'clock in the afternoon while changing channels, attempting to watch around *Three's Company* and *Family Ties*, my telephone rings twice. I usually leave my answering machine on to hear who is calling. I push the mute button on my TV remote control, the stop button of my answering machine, and pick up the receiver.

"Yes, hello, Phil," I say, and pause, listening for sounds in the background. "How is Connie?" I ask, because I can't hear anything, though I know she must be home from work.

Phil explains to me that their bathtub faucet is now leaking worse than ever, and since it's the first of the month today, he suggests I come by and take a look.

"See what can be done about it once and for all," he adds.

I tell him that I have pencilled it in for the weekend, and that I'd see him then. I glance out my living room window: the sky over the city is still dark and pouring down rain.

"It was bad before," says Phil, "leaking sporadically, but since Connie and I showered this afternoon, hot water has been steadily dripping out."

"Connie and you had a shower," I say.

"Yes," he says, "and I haven't gotten a thing done since." He pauses, and in the background, I hear a big floppy page of a newspaper turn. "My study is next to the bathroom and it's too distracting."

I tell Phil I will come over. I tell him that I will leave my house in ten minutes.

He assures me that both he and Connie will be home all evening. "It's a miserable day," he says. We say goodbye and hang up.

I turn the TV off, and re-activate my answering machine. Then I light a cigarette and watch the rain. The encyclopedias, still packed in their boxes, are stacked in the corner of my living room, next to the window.

Before opening the front door to leave, I call up the staircase to my mother, who is in her bedroom, to tell her I am going out, but I doubt she hears above the crackling of the movie projector. I was brought up in movies. My mother had been an extra in over two hundred and fifty films throughout the '40s, '50s and '60s. She could never understand why anyone would want to be a star.

It's nearly 4:40 when I pull into a spot in the rear of the building. The curtains are drawn in all but the corner apartment on the top floor. A man standing in the window whom I recognize as Phil raises a beer bottle in his right hand, and I wave up to him.

I use my pass-key and take the rear flight of stairs. I walk quickly to the end of the corridor and give their door three light raps. A toilet flushes and a woman's voice calls, "Come in," but the door opens before my hand reaches the knob, and Phil invites me into the living room.

Phil's typewriter sits in the centre of the room with its cover open; a few crumpled Kleenexes are scattered about the light brown rug. He shakes my hand and tells me he is glad I could make it. He offers me the couch, so I sit down on the middle cushion. The open newspaper is on the floor to my right.

"Can I get you a beer, Dimitri?" he asks, as he steps over the typewriter and stands at the entrance to the kitchen.

"No, thanks," I say, and spot the ashtray on the floor beside the Entertainment Section.

Phil sits in the armchair next to the telephone, his beer beside him on the table. "Wait," he says. "Listen." He stares down at the phone. He points up to the ceiling and closes his eyes. "Can you hear it?"

A door opens from down the hall, but I know that's not it, that's not the sound he means.

"It's your toilet re-filling," I say. "It's a natural sound." I pull a cigarette out and light it.

Connie enters the living room wearing her orange terrycloth bathrobe and no socks. I stand to greet her.

"You must be Dimitri," she says, and she looks over her shoulder at Phil.

"We've spoken on the phone," I say, and we shake hands.

"Yes," says Connie. "I remember."

Phil is still pointing to the ceiling. He cocks his head to one side. "That damn patter," he says. "It's driving me crazy."

Outside, the gusting wind blows a light sheet of rain against the living room window.

I offer Connie a cigarette and she takes it from my pack. We sit down together on the couch, and she tells me I am much younger than she imagined from my voice on the phone, and from what Phil had said.

"Why do I think landlords are all old and crotchety?"

"Actually," I say to her, "I don't really own the building, just manage it. The tenants, I mean. It's kind of mechanical that way."

Phil gets up from the chair and steps over his typewriter. "Can you hear it?" he says, turning toward the hallway.

I strike a match and hold it out for Connie. "My mother owns several buildings," I say, and Connie looks up at me while lighting her cigarette.

Phil stands near the living room entrance, and Connie's eyes follow him, but her head remains stationary. "You're not taking Dimitri in there, are you?" she asks.

Phil turns to face Connie and me on the couch. "I'll open the window. I want him to see the leak," he says and makes a gesture with his open hand in my direction.

"I think I hear it, Phil," I say. I pick up the ashtray and

I CAN FIX ANYTHING

hold it out for Connie. "Sort of a dripping sound."

"Yes," he says. "That's it." He turns and walks off down the hall toward the bathroom.

Connie and I are face to face. "He's right, you know. He'll go nuts." She glances over her shoulder, then looks into my face again. "It's happened before. It's all so damn predictable."

The bathroom door closes and I peer down the hall.

"Do you think he heard?" she says.

Phil is nowhere in sight.

"No," I say.

"I love him," she says. She takes a drag on her smoke and exhales. "Listen," she says, "you're a nice man."

I nod, then tap the ash from my cigarette. She tells me it is obvious that I care deeply for all my tenants, and I tell her that's true, in a sense, but I have trouble maintaining the building.

"I can fix anything," I say, "but it's the motivation that I find difficult."

She puts out her cigarette before she's smoked half, and looks to her left, to Phil's typewriter on the floor. "That's why I feel like a movie tonight," she says, and I look at her, inquisitively. "Everything's falling apart in a predictable way," she continues, "and I don't have the motivation to do anything but spectate."

We sit in silence for a moment, both of us staring at Phil's typewriter.

"Well," I say, "maybe a drink would be nice." I blow smoke toward the centre of their living room.

I CAN FIX ANYTHING

Connie gets up from the couch, steps over the typewriter, and begins mixing drinks at the kitchen table.

The toilet flushes again, and the tank begins refilling itself. Connie opens the fridge door and takes a metal ice-cube tray from the freezer. She holds it on the table firmly with her left hand, and pulls up on the lever with her right. Her movements have intentions about them, but I can't be more specific.

"What we have here seems to be a natural situation." I pause and drag on my cigarette. "A normal, everyday series of events."

I watch Connie at the table across the room, her hair falling in a gentle wave and forming the perfect point of a heart on her back, just below her shoulders. I ask myself, What is my motivation here?

She returns with the drinks.

"I don't know what I can do," I say. "What can I do?"

She hands me one of the tall glasses. "Fix it," she says. "Fix it because you're the landlord, Phil needs the job, and I'll go crazy."

The bathroom door opens. I get up from the couch and kneel in front of the typewriter. I set my drink on the light brown rug.

Connie steps around the typewriter and me, and stands by the window, her back against the sill. She guides the ashtray over the rug with her left foot, pushing it into a convenient position next to my glass. She picks up a Kleenex from the floor, then takes it from between her toes. She squeezes it into her fist. She's watching me.

I CAN FIX ANYTHING

Phil enters the living room and kneels on one knee beside me, to my left.

"A problem with your print unit, I see," I say.

"Yes," says Phil, then his voice jumps an octave. "Do you know these machines?" He raises his eyebrow and looks to Connie. Connie sets her glass on the window sill, then puts her hands into the big orange pockets of her bathrobe. She crosses her bare feet.

Phil stands up. "So it's not really broken," he says. He sits down on the arm of the big chair, and raises a finger to his lips. "Just stalled," he says.

I tell him that it *is* broken, not stalled. "But the problem is minor," I say. I reach for my glass and take a sip.

". . . because I need to type this resumé for tomorrow," he continues, and I don't know whether he has heard me.

The living room is quiet as I lean over the typewriter. In the air around me are the smells of Ivory soap and shampoo. Connie and Phil stare at each other from across the room as if they're trying to read each others' minds, though I'm not sure they're communicating.

I set my drink on the carpet next to the typewriter and get to my feet. I look at Phil, then at Connie.

"I've seen this kind of thing before," I say. "Things wear out." I look down at the typewriter. "But we're only human, right?"

They both nod. Phil takes his beer from beside the telephone and finishes the last of the foam.

"Can you fix it?" asks Connie. She uncrosses her feet and

kicks at another of the crumpled Kleenexes.

I try for a thoughtful expression, and nod my head. "But I'll need my tools," I say.

"This is great, Dimitri," says Phil, guiding me towards the apartment door. "I really need this job." He leans closer and winks. "Especially now." He nods towards the living room where Connie rests against the window sill, sipping her drink.

I leave their apartment and go downstairs to my car. When I open the trunk, I glance up to their window and stare for a moment at Connie's back. I see a big heart in the centre of the window.

The rain rattles off the open trunk as I lean in and open my toolbox. I select a tiny flathead screwdriver, a pair of needlenose pliers, a small plastic bottle containing various springs and washers, and tuck them in my coat pocket. Then I slam the trunk closed and prepare to run for shelter. Connie raises her glass and I wave up to her, the rain showering against my face.

Phil is waiting at their apartment door by the time I reach the top of the stairs.

"This is great, Dimitri," he says. He takes one long stride towards me and shakes my hand again.

"You'll be typing in ten minutes," I say, and walk past him into the living room.

"Wonderful," he says, following close behind me. "I'll owe you one."

I sit on the floor in front of his typewriter. Connie sits to my right, cross-legged. Phil kneels on one knee to my left. I pick up my screwdriver and point to the print unit, explaining the stretched and twisted spring beneath the ribbon cartridge; how it's a result of repeatedly installing correction tapes incorrectly.

"You do it enough times the wrong way," I say to them both, "this is bound to happen."

Phil leans closer, looking into his typewriter. He nods his head, slowly, as if understanding. "Connie put in the last correction tape," he says. "I remember now." He looks up. "Or, it could have been me."

I glance at Connie. "I'm not a woman of letters," she says.

Phil concentrates again on his typewriter. "What did we do wrong?" he says.

I begin to show them the correct procedure by first moving the entire print unit to the far left of the platen. I continue explaining to Phil while Connie takes her drink over to the couch and sets it on the speaker box. She moves the Entertainment Section into position on the floor.

Phil returns to his favourite chair and carefully watches my every move around his typewriter, though I can't tell if he's paying attention.

I select a new spring from the plastic container. Connie picks up her felt pen and continues stroking x's through movie ads.

"Super, Dimitri," says Phil, leaning forward.

Once I have the ribbon cartridge removed, the replacement of the spring takes only a minute. I discard the old one in the ashtray.

I stand up with my drink and finish the last sip.

"Thanks," says Connie, glancing up from the paper.

I CAN FIX ANYTHING

Phil slides from the chair and flips the lid of his typewriter closed, then carries the machine off down the hall towards his study, without a word. Within minutes we hear typing.

I tilt my glass back and forth, watching the ice cubes circle around the bottom, and Connie becomes distracted. She looks up from her paper, checking the clock on the wall above the armchair. She stands, walks to the window, then looks back at me.

I gather up my tools, waiting for her to say something. She turns away, continues looking out the window beyond the rear lot. A circular patch of fog forms on the pane in front of her face and her reflection slowly fades. I become flushed with the thought that beneath her bathrobe she is naked. My ears redden, so I run my forefinger between my neck and shirt-collar, trying to lose the thought.

Phil is typing at a steady, even pace; the patter of the keys echoes down the hall and scatters about the living room. I slip my tools into my coat pocket and begin fastening the buttons, but my fingers stumble over each one. I'm hoping Connie will turn around and remind me of the leaking faucet down the hall, but she doesn't. Instead, she asks me out to a movie.

"Which movie?" I ask.

"It doesn't matter," she says. "We can decide in your car."

I walk down the hall and into the Emersons' bathroom. Leaning over the closed toilet seat and reaching beneath the white porcelain tank, I'm able to shut off the main hot water valve. The bathroom is silent except for the steady typing from the next room.

I CAN FIX ANYTHING

As I leave the bathroom, I pause a moment. To my right, the door to Phil's study, to my left, further down the hall, I hear Connie in the bedroom. She dresses in a pair of jeans, a big wool sweater, and some warm socks. I rap lightly on Phil's door and speak into the crack between the door and its frame. "All fixed," I say.

"Thanks," he says, and continues typing.

"I'll see you later in the month," he says. "About the rent."

Connie pauses by their apartment door. She's watching me approach from down the hall. "I'm leaving now, Phil," she says, looking at me. "I'll see you later."

The typing persists. "Goodbye," says Phil.

I unlock the car door for Connie and she gets in the passenger side. I get in behind the wheel and start the engine. The interior begins to warm at once so Connie removes her boots and rests her feet next to the heating vent.

"Sometimes," she says, slouching further down in her seat, staring out the side window, "I feel like a movie, and away I go." She glances over at me with the very beginning of a smile on her lips.

"I know a good one," I say, switching on the headlights and wipers. "I've seen them all, and I know how they end. That way, it's easier to know the good ones."

Connie is content. Phil is content. And I am behind the wheel.

KING KONG

SAMUEL GOLDWYN PROduced a movie about a legendary ape living on a legendary island. *King Kong: The Eighth Wonder of the World* is written in tall, bold letters on the Broadway marquee.

The movie begins in Hoboken with a producer named Carl Denham. Denham is checking out the soup line for a woman to play the lead. He can't find one there, so he goes to an all-night café somewhere in New York City. A beautiful woman catches his eye in this unlikely place. He walks over and asks if she wants to be a star. He tells her he's going on a voyage in the morning to an island somewhere far, far away and she can be the star of this new movie if only she will come along. Her eyes open round and wide. She's unable to answer at first, but a star is just what she wants to be.

I CAN FIX ANYTHING

"It won't be no picnic . . . ," says Denham.

"Oh . . ."

" . . . so don't kid yourself, sister."

Her name is Ann Darrow (played by Fay Wray), and she is a classic pre-Second World War beauty. Blonde hair, wavy, and framing the contours of her face. Falling down around her soft neck. Softer than the *oo* in smooth.

The next morning, on the ship, the entire crew is apprehensive about having a woman on board. They say things like, "What's the poop on the dame, Captain?" and "We run into high seas, it'll be lights out and dame over." Jack Driscol, the strapping young first mate with shoulders bigger than Chicago's, jumps to Ann's defence.

"Lay off the broad, Scully."

The captain has no choice but to confine Ann to the hold until they reach the island. She finds a cute little spider monkey and instantly takes a liking to it. Carl Denham comes in and finds the two playing below. "Beauty and the beast," he says. He repeats it over and over again. "Beauty and the beast. Beauty and the beast. That's what this film is about."

Goldwyn and his director, Cecil B. DeMille, stand off the set. Fay joins them, and tries to explain that the scene in the ship's hold is very ambiguous.

"Who's to say a spider monkey is any less beautiful than a woman?" she argues. "Or vice versa? A woman is a woman and a monkey is a monkey. To other monkeys, there lies its beauty. Comparing two mutually exclusive creatures is absurd."

Samuel smiles into Fay's deep blue eyes. DeMille reminds Miss Wray, "You're not being paid to analyze contrasting principles or to undermine the script department. You're here to act."

❂

Fay Wray's boyfriend is a young man named Hendrix Wells. He's having a tough time maintaining his normal life, trying to begin his writing career and staying in love with Fay all at the same time. He loves her madly. Hendrix has moved into Fay's small apartment while she's away making her first big movie, and he dreams of her every day, washing her dishes, making her bed, straightening up, dusting. But he's bitter. "I don't trust my Uncle Sam as far as I can throw one of his stunt men," he said on the New York dock after he kissed Fay goodbye.

❂

"Confound fog!" screams the captain. He and his crew attempt to navigate their way to the shore of the island, relying on the decreasing depth to tell them how near they are.

"Thirty fathoms, Captain."
"Thicker than pappy's tattoos, this fog."
"Twenty fathoms, Sir."

The fog mysteriously dissipates and they see the mountain that resembles a skull—Skull Mountain. They make their way ashore, and as they trudge through the dense jungle toward the fortified village, they hear the natives chanting. Carl Denham, who leads the way, interprets the chant as a welcome. The cameramen zoom in on the main gate. "Listen, they've seen us and they're welcoming us," says Denham. He points through the tropical foliage toward the village gates. "They're saying, 'Come. Come. Come.'"

"Kong. Kong. Kong," say the natives.

Beyond the frame of the picture, Fay gently elbows Mr. Goldwyn in the ribs and says, "Perhaps they just want to be stars." She winks.

Hendrix leaves the apartment on Saturday morning to do the laundry. He drives a Model A, as everyone did back then. The gas gauge, speedometer, and turn signals do not function. He hands his laundry, along with a few of Fay's things she left behind, to the woman who operates the laundromat and returns to his car, where he retrieves a hard-cover notebook from the passenger seat and begins to write. He's working on a novel about a young guy who had it all—money, a good name, a good family background—but wanted to be a writer. Hendrix's hero left his home in Eureka, California, and moved to New York where he couldn't find a job but met a struggling young actress in an all-night café, with whom he hit it off instantly. The two young artists shared stories about what it was like to come to a big city, and dreams about what it must be like to become famous. Chapter One is as far as he's gotten.

In that all-night café, Hendrix told Fay that his uncle was the famous movie producer, Samuel Goldwyn. Hendrix suggested that he talk to his uncle about a screen test. "I can't guarantee anything."

"I would appreciate it, Hendrix," she said, "but I've heard stories about famous Hollywood producers."

"He's very influential." Hendrix was nonchalant, as he sipped his coffee and gazed across the small round table, but he saw that Fay was impressed.

✦

The film crew has returned to the ship, which is anchored in Skull Lagoon, and is filming the next scene between Jack and Ann. Jack says, "I . . . I love ya, Ann. Is there? . . . Do ya . . . do ya feel anything, something like that, to me?"

Suspense. She looks at him. He looks at her. They've only known each other three days. Then she smiles. They embrace in the soft grey shadows of the upper deck, and he kisses her on the top lip and she kisses him on the bottom lip. They make plans for when they return to the States.

Jack is called to the bridge by the captain, and Ann decides to stay on deck for a little while. "Such a beautiful night," she says. "All the stars are out."

✦

Hendrix stares at the blank page of his notebook for a few more minutes, then throws it and the pencil to the passenger-side floor. The pencil slides across the hard cover and slips

I CAN FIX ANYTHING

through a rust hole in the floorboard. It rolls across the pavement, and as Hendrix leaves the car he steps on it, breaking it in half. He heads down to the hot-dog stand and buys a Coke. Walking back to his car, he tries to figure out how he can work this into his novel. About how two people strike up a great relationship because they have so many things in common, but then one of them gets a real break and leaves, promising to always come home and to always keep things as they always were. That person vows to stay in love but the person who's left behind can't help but worry, because Tinseltown is so very tempting with all its glamour and parties. Lately, Hendrix has found it increasingly more difficult to fit anything that happens into his novel. He thinks about Fay and, in turn, his Uncle Sam, and about how Uncle's eyes lit up at Fay's screen test before she even opened her mouth. Fay had left the set when Hendrix went to face his uncle. He proclaimed that she was his, the only woman he'd ever loved.

"But perhaps I could write a script," he says to the people on the sidewalk. "A movie script. And perhaps I could make up with Uncle and he could get me a real break." The people on the sidewalk nod in agreement as they pass him.

He reaches the rear parking lot of the laundromat, and stands for a moment, gazing at the lug nuts on the left rear wheel of his car. His mind returns to the New York dock. His mind has made a lot of return visits to the waterfront since he said "Goodbye" and "I love you" to Fay. He searches laid-yards and explores the huge warehouses that line the shore. He finds himself being drawn to them at night. He goes for walks during the shortest hours of the morning.

Hendrix retrieves his clean laundry and gets into his car. He begins to think about Fay and, in turn, how he should apologize to his uncle.

❂

In the shadow of Skull Mountain the natives are preparing for a ceremony. They kidnapped Ann in an earlier scene, and now she's tied by her wrists and ankles, almost suspended, between two idols, which look more like West Coast Indian totem poles, but she doesn't know that. The actual tying up of Fay wasn't put on film. It was cut from the script by Mr. DeMille (upon Goldwyn's request) just before shooting. Uncle Sam tied Fay's ankles and wrists to the statues. He checked with her twice, very carefully both times, to ensure that the rope was neither too coarse nor too tight.

Mr. Goldwyn takes his place behind the director's chair and lifts his hands into the air as if he were a fruit vendor showing two prize cantaloupes, which is a signal to Fay for more screaming, more fright. Encouragement from Goldwyn comes in addition to that of Mr. DeMille. Ann screams for her life.

The natives charge back to their walled city, close the huge gates, and wait restlessly inside. They hope their sacrifice will suffice.

Ann tries to be brave but she's afraid, and with good reason, because here comes the giant manlike ape. While the camera trains in on Kong, Ann winces to herself: the loose twine is twisting around her wrists, chafing at her supple skin. King Kong frees Ann and makes off with his *Golden Prize*.

✪

Hendrix runs out of gas backing his car from the parking spot and inadvertently rolls into the entrance driveway of the laundromat. The woman from the laundromat comes out and begins screaming. One of her hands is locked around a crowbar.

He tries to explain: "My gas gauge is broken. I was lower than I thought."

She doesn't want excuses. She wants that car out of here. "It's blocking my driveway," she yells.

Hendrix begins walking to the nearest gas station, three blocks down and on the other side of the street. He thinks of his girl, and what she must be doing now.

✪

DeMille directs Jack Driscol, Carl Denham, and his film crew as they track Kong. He's heading for the high ground, as apes will do when being pursued. He's heading for Skull Mountain. The men come to a lake with no way across. Kong took the raft. They unsnag a beached log and pile onto it, but there is yet another snag to this method of chase: a brontosaurus lives in this lake, and sure enough there it is, lifting its head from the depths, capsizing the log. Many men die trying to make it to shore, but Jack and Carl scramble to safety. Once

KING KONG

back on land, they move skillfully through the dense and unfamiliar terrain. They're gaining on Kong.

❂

Hendrix returns with the gas just in time to stop the Empire Towing Company from removing his car. He tries to put the nozzle of the bleach bottle into his tank, but it won't fit. The gas station didn't have a small enough gas can. He thinks for a moment while the crowbar slices the air, and the woman yells from the rear entrance of her laundromat. Hendrix is still thinking about Fay out in Hollywood, or were they shooting this picture on location? He can't remember much. He does remember the Coke bottle in his car, so he runs to retrieve it.

But instead, he's running along the waterfront. Blackness. He sees nothing and hears only the muffled screams of Fay. They call from the darkness, from one of the warehouses. But which one? He hears men's voices beneath the cries of his beloved.

❂

Jack and Carl have caught up to Kong but stay out of sight, waiting in bushes while the chivalrous ape protects Ann from the tyrannosaurus rex. He's boxing it. Kong feigns a body punch, then attacks with a right to the head, a left, and the rex is down. Kong leaps on the beast and bites its neck. The rex is dead. Ann screams from where she lies near a huge boulder, where Kong set her down for safety. Kong spots Jack

I CAN FIX ANYTHING

and Carl, so he picks her up and moves her nearer the cliff. He lays her down and leaves to battle his relentless pursuers.

DeMille motions for a cameraman to zoom in on the pterodactyl as it dives down from somewhere above the tree tops, screeching towards Ann. Its talons open to seize.

But before it can clutch Ann in its fatal grip, Kong turns in the nick and snatches the reptilian bird from mid-flight, breaks it cleanly in half, snapping its hollow bones, and throws it over the bluff. Everybody on Skull Island wants Ann for themselves but Kong wants her more and he's the toughest, he's the king. A huge stegosaurus, built low to the ground, lumbers into the clearing. Kong leaps to Ann's defence, but he's forgotten about Jack and Carl. Jack sneaks around the battleground (behind the cameras) and lowers himself onto a narrow ledge approximately ten feet below the lip of the cliff. He inches along slowly, his back against the stone, his arms searching for niches, cracks, and crevices. He looks to the river, far below, then to his rope, then to Ann. She is perched directly above him, screaming for her life.

Goldwyn is lifting cantaloupes off camera.

When Jack makes it to the ledge, he secures his rope to a stump, and the hero and heroine lower themselves into the cool safety of the river.

❂

Hendrix holds the neck of the Coke bottle and breaks off the bottom half by smashing it against the hard edge of a cement retaining wall at the entrance to the laundromat. He puts the

KING KONG

lip of the severed bottle into his gas tank, using the neck as a funnel. Smiling at his ingenuity, he thinks of his love for Fay and his contempt for his uncle. He tosses the empty bleach bottle aside and reaches into his breast pocket for his car keys.

Instead, he pulls a snub-nosed .38 from his shoulder holster and blows apart the padlock, yanks the match from between his teeth, and kicks in the door. There is a light in the corner of the warehouse. Three dark figures crowd around an illuminated one. The three silhouettes lower their arms and turn toward Hendrix—Uncle Sam and the two Warner brothers.

"Let's get'im, boys," says Jack Warner.

"No one's taking what's ours," says Harry.

Uncle Sam doesn't say anything. He just starts walking slowly toward his nephew, and the Warners assume flanking positions, Jack on Sam's right, Harry on his left.

Hendrix raises his pistol and says, "Untie Fay, Uncle, or would you rather I tuck you in for the big sleep? The choice is yours."

Uncle Sam and the Warners continue toward Hendrix. Fay crouches down against her drainpipe. She cries softly. Harry Warner picks up a metal rod and slaps it into his left palm.

"I don't think I'm the one with the choice, Hendrix, my boy," says Uncle Sam.

Slap, slap.

Hendrix knew his uncle was up to no good. Look at poor Fay tied to that cold pipe.

I CAN FIX ANYTHING

"You see," says Sam, his hands suddenly in the air, "we're not alone." Six men instantly emerge from behind oil barrels. Goldwyn's hands fall calmly to his sides once more.

Slap, slap.

All six men converge on Hendrix. He turns and fires. He wheels and shoots. He rolls and squeezes the trigger. He somersaults and blasts. He vaults and snipes. He pivots on his heel and discharges his final round. All six men lie with wounded left thighs. Hendrix's .38 clicks empty and its barrel smokes. He throws it at Goldwyn, but Uncle Sam ducks and Jack Warner takes the snub-nose on the forehead and is knocked out cold. Harry jumps with his pipe cutting through the air. Hendrix grabs a Coke bottle by the neck and smashes the bottom against the cement floor. The pipe glances by Hendrix's head as he slashes out with his glass, catching Harry's right forearm. The pipe hits the floor first and Harry crumples alongside it.

Uncle Sam moves closer.

Kong beats at the gates of the native city. Within its walls there's chaos, confusion. Natives are running everywhere. The chief calls to his shaman for advice. The shaman tells him there is only one way to appease the beast. They must, once again, surrender *The Golden Girl* to Kong.

Jack Driscol won't have it. He loves Ann ("The only dame I ever loved!") and would rather die himself than give her up to some ape.

Kong bursts through the gates, searching for his prize amid the commotion. Carl Denham is racing back to the ship. He has a plan. He returns just as Kong closes in on Ann, who has raced from hut to hut and now stands clinging to Jack, her back against the village wall.

Denham returns and begins lobbing gas bombs at the giant ape. One, then another, and the King falls to the ground, knocked senseless by the blasts, the smoke, and the shock.

While Kong is still unconscious, the remaining crew load him into the cargo hold and secure him for the voyage back to New York. It appears that more men actually survived Lake Brontosaurus than first estimated, or perhaps the men securing Kong are the ship's crew, and are not to be confused with the film crew.

Hendrix primes the carburetor and fires up his Model A. He's finally able to leave the laundromat parking lot, so he drives back to Fay's apartment. He's got the old warehouse on his mind but he's working on a different sequence of events.

"I should be writing this down," he says, closing the door to Fay's apartment.

Suddenly he and Fay are trapped on the roof of the tallest warehouse on the waterfront. The place is surrounded by cops and newspaper people. Uncle Sam's voice is louder and more threatening through the megaphone.

Hendrix turns to his girl. Her blonde hair is nudged into the golden stream of the searchlight by a gentle Atlantic breeze. Her blue eyes are almost crying, almost surrendering.

"Listen, toots," Hendrix says, "they think it's just me up here. I'll give myself up. You wait 'til the coast is clear, then high-tail it to California. I'll catch up with you in Eureka once I'm cleared of this bum rap."

Fay gazes up at him, then past him to the stars.

"I shouldn't have trusted him," says Hendrix. "Uncle Sam is up to no good."

Fay pleads: "But, he'll . . . he'll . . . "

Then she punctuates her pleas with a passionate kiss. He struggles a bit at first then subsides. He kisses her upper, she his lower.

✪

Kong is chained to a huge wooden cross that the ship's crew constructed from thick trees found on Skull Island. The spider monkey dances around Kong's mighty feet, and the giant ape cries softly for his lost prize.

On deck, Carl Denham expresses his excitement and explains to Jack and Ann that they will all be world-famous for capturing *The Eighth Wonder of the World*. Then he leaves the lovers alone. They fall into each other's arms and whisper dreamily to each other about their forthcoming marriage.

"Cut, and . . . that's a print," says Mr. DeMille. Then he leaves the set. He seems always in a huff about one thing or another. He feels compromised and manipulated, but he doesn't know what else he can do.

"Thank you, people. Supper, everyone. Take forty-five."

The assistant director puts down his clipboard, and the set relaxes.

Cecil B. DeMille enters the galley, and Mr. Goldwyn speaks to his director from across the room. "How about *Son of Kong* or *Return to Skull Island*?"

"Both are good titles, Sam," says Cecil, as he takes a place at the same table. "But we'll have to see how the New York sequences shoot in this picture. I'm worried about the final scene."

"On the Empire State Building?"

"Yes."

"Fay will be wonderful."

"There's a lot of screaming."

"She'll be wonderful, Cecil, don't worry."

The actors, actresses, technicians, cameramen, and film crew enter the galley. Mr. Goldwyn motions for Fay to come sit with him.

"I'm looking forward to getting back to New York," says Fay.

"Haven't you enjoyed yourself, my dear?"

"Oh yes, but I miss my boyfriend madly. And I want to get on with my career."

"But this is your career."

"It's a beginning, true, but I have to move on, and up."

"Mr. DeMille and I were just talking about your next film."

"My next . . . "

"Nothing was settled," says Cecil, between mouthfuls of

mashed potatoes. "We still have to finish the New York sequences on *this* film."

"I'm going to make you a star, Miss Wray."

"Oh, Uncle Sam."

❂

Hendrix has rolled his sleeping bag up and taken it to the dock where the motion picture crew will be landing tomorrow. He knows every warehouse and every laid-yard along the waterfront.

He spreads his bedroll out behind a dormant forklift not far from the waves. He removes his wallet and car keys from his pocket and his snub-nose from his shoulder holster and lays them by his head.

"Uncle Sam ain't taking what's mine, or hers, or ours." He pauses a moment lying on his back, gazing up into the clear, dark sky full of stars. "Uncle Sam ain't taking anything, whosever it is." Hendrix tries to fall asleep.

❂

"Oh, Uncle Sam, doesn't the Statue of Liberty look wonderful through the mist?"

"Yes, and so do you."

"Uncle," says Fay, rolling her eyes, "it's kind of spooky, though. Like if you didn't know it was there, or what it was. It's so big and mysterious."

"Yes, but you don't have to call me Uncle. Just call me Sam."

"Oh, but I might as well get used to it. Once Hendrix and I are married, what else will I call you?"

"Then he's proposed to you?"

"Well, not exactly, but we've talked about it."

"I don't know if there will be enough time for a wedding. If we begin the next picture right away, that is."

"But Hendrix and I want to . . ."

"Just postponed for a while, not called off."

"And I appreciate the opportunity you've given me, but I want to make movies that *matter*."

"Just a few months. You want to be a star, don't you, Fay?"

"Oh, yes, Uncle Sam, but Hendrix and I love each other. In fact he's probably waiting on the dock for me. See if you can see him. Look!"

✲

It isn't the first light that wakes Hendrix, it is the throng of hopeful extras for the *Broadway Theatre* scene and the *Melee in the Streets* scene. The ship is still on the horizon as Hendrix peers over the top of the forklift and through the early morning mist. He collects his keys, wallet, and gun, and puts them in their appropriate holsters. He leaves his bedroll and pushes his way through the crowd.

✲

The gangplank is lowered to the dock. Hendrix holds his front-row position, his arms out from his sides, pushing against the crowd behind him. Pens, notebooks, and eight-by-ten glossies are thrust into his peripheral vision as the extras push their way to sea, and to the real live movie stars.

Fay appears at the top of the gangplank. Uncle Sam is on her arm. She spots Hendrix in the crowd below. She abandons her bouquet and her producer, and runs to her love. Hendrix lifts her into the air and they twirl, suspended above the dock.

Uncle Sam waits for them to land, then takes a position next to Fay. He rests a hand on her shoulder.

"Hello, Hendrix, my boy. Glad you could meet us. It means a lot to Fay." He turns to face her. "We better get right over to the hotel so we can get cleaned up. We've got a full day of shooting ahead of us."

"Oh, I missed you, Fay," Hendrix says.

"Me too. Uncle Sam is going to make me a star."

"Uncle Sam?"

✪

A huge crate is unloaded from the ship and placed carefully on the dock.

✪

"Remember, Fay, tonight we shoot the *Theatre* scene."

✪

Suddenly, Hendrix throws Fay over his shoulder and makes off with her down the waterfront. Samuel Goldwyn shouts,

"After them, don't let him get away with my star."

Uncle Sam leads the charge and all the potential extras fall in behind, anxious and hopeful for roles of their own.

Hendrix ducks into the Empire & State Shipping and Storage warehouse, and his pursuers are momentarily fooled.

A young woman's face lights up and her shrill voice breaks from the crowd as she points overhead. "He's got her on the roof!"

The crowd surrounds the warehouse. Soon the entire area is moving with newspapermen, cameras, longshoremen, wives, old men and women who happen to be passing by, cops, small children, teenagers, autograph seekers, photographers, and searchlights.

Samuel Goldwyn obtains a megaphone from the district police chief, who has come down from his precinct office to personally oversee the arrival proceedings.

○

Hendrix stands atop the tallest warehouse on the waterfront with his hands gently resting upon Fay's waist.

"You're wrong, Hendrix. I *can* handle him. He only wants to make me a star. Then you and I get married." She runs her hand through his ruffled hair. "Once I'm a star."

○

"Give yourself up, Hendrix," says Goldwyn. "The place is surrounded." He motions with one arm for the police to storm the warehouse. "I don't know what you're trying to prove, my boy. Miss Wray is under contract to me."

○

A policeman lands on the ledge, then vaults himself onto the warehouse roof.

Hendrix turns and fires. The policeman falls with a flesh wound to his thigh. Hendrix lays Fay down behind a wooden crate for safety, then quickly moves across the roof to draw the gunfire away from her. She props her head up on one hand and watches the action.

In a few short moments, six policemen lay wounded and a seventh unconscious, due to a blow to the head, before Hendrix is nabbed by the police chief.

Uncle Sam helps Fay to her feet.

Hendrix is thrown in jail.

○

In the Broadway theatre, Carl Denham stands on stage with his hands in the air, silencing the crowd. A sell-out audience has gathered to see *King Kong: The Eighth Wonder of the World*.

○

Hendrix overpowers his guards and breaks out of his temporary-holding cell in Manhattan South. He steals a Model A and heads for Broadway. The cops are on his tail. Sirens fill the night.

✷

Jack Driscoll and Ann Darrow join Carl on stage, and the crowd goes wild. DeMille and Goldwyn stand together in the orchestra pit, directing and encouraging.

There's a collective gasp as the curtains begin to part to reveal the expanse of Kong's chest and mighty limbs, kept docile beneath thick iron shackles. His humiliated eyes are moist in the corners.

Flashbulbs ignite and Kong, remembering the gas bombs cast by Denham, breaks the shackle holding his right wrist. He won't be held captive a second time.

Goldwyn juggles cantaloupes in the orchestra pit.

Kong's left arm is also free and Goldwyn juggles faster.

The melee breaks from the theatre out onto the street. Kong randomly takes down telephone poles and traffic lights as he busts his way through the city streets. He peers into windows searching for his *Golden Prize*, but Jack has taken her to safety. He, Ann, and Carl are speeding their way across town to book a room in the Empire State Building, the tallest building in the world.

✷

Hendrix is heading for Broadway along Fifth Avenue. The law is shooting at Hendrix, but a moving target is hard to hit. Finally, at the corner of Thirty-fourth and Fifth, a copper's bullet enters the left rear tire of Hendrix's hot Model A. He loses control and smashes into a fire hydrant. Water springs

I CAN FIX ANYTHING

from the concrete like a geyser. He jumps from his car and runs into the lobby of the Empire State Building.

The cops follow.

✵

Kong has just derailed a subway car but there's still no Ann in sight. He makes his way down Thirty-fourth Street toward Fifth Avenue, knocking cars and buses from his path. Then, suddenly, from the huge corner of his eye, he sees his *Golden Prize*. Through a window of a twelfth-floor suite, the soft interior light dances around her hair.

Kong attains a wide ledge on the Empire State Building. Reaching a mighty hand through the window, he seizes his love, then continues his climb, heading for higher ground.

✵

The cops chase Hendrix around the first floor, then back to street level and throughout the lobby.

✵

Kong is on the summit of the Empire State Building. Ann's hair blows in the breeze while she screams into the palm of Kong's mighty hand.

The cameras zoom in on the biplanes, so Fay takes in the view from the safety of Kong's fist. She looks between his fingers and studies the city and the bustling, frantic world around her.

The fighter pilots wait for Ann to be deposited somewhere

safe so they can blast Kong. Kong waves his free hand, defending his love from the pesky planes. Then he gently sets her down on the highest ledge. He's weakening from the climb and all the commotion.

Mr. DeMille is seated in his director's chair on the corner of Fifth and Thirty-fourth. "Open fire!" he screams.

✪

The cops corral Hendrix in the lobby: his only escape is through the Fifth Avenue exit. He's crying, calling for Fay.

✪

Goldwyn's hands fly above his head and mingle with the stars.

✪

Kong's salty tears seep from his eyes, and run like forest creeks over his hairy face before falling into the open bullet wounds now dotting his chest. He moves Ann to a wider ledge. His heart cleaves, then finally breaks. Kong wavers in the breeze high above New York, and just for an instant, it seems as though he may be carried away into the starry night sky. His grip weakens, his footing unbalances, then he falls, bouncing once, twice off the Empire State Building, landing squarely on young Hendrix Wells as he flees the law, crushing him against the concrete jungle street.

✪

Cut. Print. It's a wrap.

I CAN FIX ANYTHING

❂

In the elevator, on her way down the one hundred and two storeys, Fay sits in the specially-installed swivel chair, attended by one woman from Make-up and another from Wardrobe. In her mind, she is finished with this movie, the movie which seemed at first like such a good idea (and indeed, from certain perspectives, remains a good one: it's bound to make millions, to make her a star), however, she is not in truth finished with this picture yet. The most troubling scene for Fay Wray is yet to come—the 'sentimental' scene in the street in which she grieves the loss of the once-mighty ape—but for Ann Darrow it is an easy scene with lots of emotion.

SHE MAKES
THE WORLD FLAT

THE SCOTS-PINE WALL unit is recent, and the chesterfield has been reupholstered in my sister's living room. I have been standing in front of her living room window for the past few moments, studying the old guy who still lives across the street. He braces the blade of a pruning hook against his sharpening treadle. Beyond him, his trees rank alphabetically from apple to walnut, and stretch the full length of his lot. I have not seen my sister in fifteen years, so we have never spoken of Frank's accident, and now it does not seem likely. I remember that my cigarette is smoldering in the green glass ashtray in the kitchen.

I return to her kitchen, and to my sister, and to my coffee, which I know will be cold. I sit at the table and take my cigarette from the ashtray. My sister is concentrating, poised

I CAN FIX ANYTHING

over the jigsaw puzzle, working her way through northern Italy. She fits into place a conglomerate made up of three pieces, which includes Milan, Turin, and Genoa. It has held together since the last time she and her husband assembled the puzzle, some weeks ago. My sister is very efficient at recognizing obscure villages and vague topographical features from all over the world, and equally efficient at fitting pieces into place so their patterned curves and angles accept those of the neighbouring pieces. She taps each piece of the puzzle twice with her forefinger to secure it in its place. It seems to be a habit of hers.

The deep green ashtray overflows on the table in front of me. It has remained with the house even though our parents moved. It was a Christmas gift from my sister and me when we were kids. It overflows because we both smoke heavily now.

Her kitchen appliances line the counter to the right of the sink and above the dishwasher: a digital clock/radio, an electric can-opener, a food processor, a four-slice toaster, a microwave oven, a Mixmaster on its stand, and a multi-speed blender, all fitting snugly beneath the cupboards.

When she leaves the puzzle, it's only to drink her coffee and smoke her cigarette. Our conversation crosses the broken surface of the world. Then her fingers begin again to search out the border regions of northern Italy.

"I leave the oceans to Frank," she says, then takes the last cookie. "All that blue. I don't know how he does it."

My sister is a short woman with long hair. I remember her when we were young as being as tall as me. Because she and

SHE MAKES THE WORLD FLAT

I grew at the same pace throughout her first fourteen years and my first fifteen, I assumed we would always be the same height. She did many things better than me back then, except climb trees. Frank and I were tops in tree climbing. My sister and I shared the same clothes when we were kids, and I'm sure when the three of us played in the bushes across the street, the old man thought we were all boys.

After a time she moves into the southern regions of France, pausing every few moments to sip her coffee and puff on her cigarette, not because certain pieces elude her at crucial crossroads, but because she is relaxing with her coffee. She leans back in her chair, holds her mug with both hands.

"How long have you got?" she says. Her glasses slip down her nose and her lips quiver into a slight smile. She leans forward again and, setting her coffee cup on the table in what will become the north Pacific, she continues working east to west through mainland Europe.

I tell her my plane leaves tomorrow morning.

She doesn't part her hair in the middle any more: instead, she wears bangs that fall to her eyebrows. Her hair is still very blonde, almost white. She pushes her glasses back into place.

"How's Frank?" I ask, and light a cigarette. Southern France is beginning to take shape at the tips of my sister's fingers. I sip my coffee. "I was really hoping to catch Frank at home," I say.

She holds a small piece of the Mediterranean coastline in her left hand. She hesitates. Marseille only nudges in from the top and there is mostly blue in the piece. "He's good at

I CAN FIX ANYTHING

water, and he likes doing it," she says. "I prefer the mainland." She sets the piece aside.

Her hands have aged in the years I've been away, and I wonder whether she lost it or just never wore a ring.

"Want some more cookies?" she says, standing away from the table, holding the empty plate.

"Yes," I say, "and some more coffee if you have time." The final sip of coffee is bitter cold, and I set the cup next to the green ashtray.

"Of course I have time. You're my brother, aren't you?"

It's Sunday morning; the neighbourhood is quiet. She pours more coffee. I look between the curtains, out the kitchen window. She and her kids must have installed the set of monkey bars I see in the back yard, and the lawn has been freshly cut. She works hard to keep things in order.

She sets a plate of five chocolate-chip cookies on the table in what will be the Arctic regions north of Scandinavia.

"I'll empty that," she says, and takes the ashtray. "Did you always part your hair on that side?"

The question comes from right out of the blue, and yet seems so insignificant that I wonder what she really wants to know. She sits down again, and we light cigarettes.

I notice the crack along the bottom of the green ashtray and the chipped corner when she drops in our match. It seems we should have so much to say, but we don't talk about anything.

"What do you think about the Iberian Peninsula next," she says, and looks at the envelopes propped against the window sill in front of her.

SHE MAKES THE WORLD FLAT

"There's a lot of coastline," I say.

She takes a break from the puzzle with just one piece remaining to complete southern France. Her arms are crossed on the edge of the table as she leans forward.

"I've been here before," I say, and she tilts her head to look at me and straightens her posture. "Last year about this time, I was in town, rented a car, and drove out. It didn't look like anyone was home."

She unfolds her arms and motions toward the refrigerator.

"We were vacationing. It was Frank's idea to take the kids to the coast. He took that picture from the seawall."

A heart-shaped magnet fastens a photograph of my sister and her two small children to the fridge. The two kids, a boy and a girl, my nephew and niece, wave to the camera, but my sister sees something farther down the beach, that causes her to look away. There is some sky and some sand, but mostly there is ocean above the three heads and the waving hands. They remind me of us, naturally, brother and sister.

I look away from the fridge and pull one of the curtains along its rod, achieving a wider view. The neighbouring back yards contain lawn chairs, log formations, monkey bars, picnic tables, sandboxes, and teeter-totters.

My sister sips her coffee, and we both reach for the same cookie.

"Go ahead," she says.

I nibble on the cookie, then place it on the table beside my coffee cup.

She then completes southern France by inserting the final

piece, which contains a tiny country I have never heard of, Andorra, set in the central Pyrenees. She reaches for the envelope marked *Northern France*, dumps the pieces on the table, and begins turning them right side up.

"You see the yard with the red and white lawn chairs?" She taps the ash from her cigarette into the green ashtray.

The yard is three lots away on the same side of the street, attached to a blue house and contained by a white fence. My sister is unable to see the yard from her end of the table, but she knows the area, and besides, she's busy. I stare out the window.

"Frank and I figure that's where the three of us had our fort when we were kids," she says, then continues flipping the pieces. "Remember?"

But I'm not sure I do remember.

"Our secret fort," she says. "It was right where they're now assembling the aluminum shed."

"We had lots of forts, and all of them were secret," I say. "That was the point." I toy with my cookie, move it around in a tight circle on the table with my forefinger. "How can you remember?"

"Mother and Father took the apartment the year Frank and I got married." She blows smoke across the puzzle. "We watched those houses being built, so we couldn't help but keep track of things."

"I remember the fort across the street," I say. "In the bush behind the old man's orchard."

"There," she says, once she has flipped the last piece of the

SHE MAKES THE WORLD FLAT

Brittany coastline. "Rouen is west of Paris, right?"

"I wonder if it's still there. That fort behind the old man's orchard. It was so well concealed."

The bottom of the green ashtray is dusted with grey and black ash.

"We don't call it an orchard anymore. It's just a bunch of fruit trees."

I nod, because technically I suppose she is correct.

"The night you and Frank planned to sleep out and got caught in the plum tree," says my sister, and she focuses on me for just an instant.

"The plum trees are at the centre of his orchard," I say. "We pulled lots of raids, too."

She suddenly looks very serious as she holds a piece of the English Channel that has obviously slipped into the wrong envelope.

"Who would've thought the old man would follow?" I say. "Frank and I climbed as high as we could."

"I wasn't allowed in that fort," says my sister, and her voice teeters. She tosses the piece toward the window sill. "That was yours and Frank's. And I wasn't allowed."

"I would have let you in," I say, and reach for my coffee cup.

"You don't blame Frank for anything." She stabs her cigarette into the bottom of the green ashtray. There's a short tail of grey smoke, and we both watch it rise silently toward the ceiling. The refrigerator hums, and I can't decide if she is asking or telling me.

I CAN FIX ANYTHING

"No, of course not," I say. "I don't blame anyone."

A long pause begins, perhaps fifteen or twenty minutes pass, and almost all of France is intact before either of us speak.

On the window sill above the kitchen sink there are three yellow tulips in a plain glass vase. At the end of the arborite counter, the black phone still hangs on the wall, but it has been lowered and is now even with the countertop. I look away and light another cigarette, then balance it on the chipped corner of the green ashtray.

I stand up, loosen my tie, and go into the living room. There are three worn spots in the carpet before the wall unit, wherein a collection of books, several family photos, a collection of records, a reel-to-reel tape unit, a hi-fi stereo, and a tv all occupy the many shelves of the Scots-pine framework. I have entered the living room to look out my sister's front window.

The sky is blue, and the trees cast sturdy shadows from across the street, over my sister's front yard, and almost to my feet. The paths we made leading into the bush have long since grown over, and the houses surrounding our forest make it even denser and much greener than I have remembered. Across the street, the old man is working his treadle, sharpening his tools. My sister's window is clean except toward the bottom, near the wooden sill where handprints, too small to be Frank's, smudge the pane. The blade grinds against the whetstone but there are no sparks.

"How is Frank?" I call back to the kitchen. "I mean, how's he managing?"

My sister is flipping Germany right-side-up when I sit at

SHE MAKES THE WORLD FLAT

the table again and take my cigarette from the ashtray. It has burned nearly all away.

"He's managing," she says, and then she looks right at me again. "Would you like to begin South America?"

It seems like a small enough continent, but big enough at the same time to make an impression on the rest of the world before Frank gets home with the kids.

"I'm not very good at puzzles," I say. "Except maybe those ones made for kids." I reach for the envelope marked *South America* and pour out a series of smaller envelopes, some marked with single countries, but most with two or three. Especially the northern envelopes. I choose Argentina because the Falkland Islands were in the news a few years ago.

"Stop at the coastlines, though." She returns to mainland Europe. "The oceans are for Frank."

"You know," I say, "I think it's great how you and Frank work on this puzzle together."

She takes a long puff and inhales deeply. My sister has raised her head, and she is looking straight out the kitchen window. "I'll close my eyes tonight," she says, and she closes her eyes, "and I'll see the world flat, and broken into tiny pieces." The smoke slips from her nose and mouth in irregular clouds as she speaks. "It always happens, whether we're making the puzzle or not," she says. She opens her eyes and returns to the puzzle.

We work on our separate continents in our own corners of the world, and when I finish Argentina (it consists of only nine pieces) I am pleased but at the same time disappointed

I CAN FIX ANYTHING

because I have used all nine, and still there are no Falklands. I ask my sister: "What about the Falklands?" And she tells me that if any island is not clearly visible from the mainland, it belongs to the ocean. I am pleased nonetheless.

"At least," she says, pausing over a piece containing the northeast corner of Munich and only a hint of the Danube, "I didn't offer you Australia."

I'm not sure what she means by this but I think she's smiling, and I'm excited to be helping, so I reach for another envelope.

"Chile next," I say, but my sister has backed away from the world and stands between the stove and fridge, leaning against the short counter on which the coffee maker sits alongside the spice rack that I made when I was fourteen. A long ash falls from her cigarette and she scatters it across the floor tile with a quick kick, and I see that she is not smiling. My sister's eyes are blue.

I take the green ashtray from the table and hold it out for her, but she ignores it. Her arms are tightly folded across her stomach and she stares out the kitchen window above the sink at nothing specific, but at something.

"Frank will be home soon," she says. "The kids get bored with him and he gets tired."

I'm standing between my sister and the kitchen table, holding the heavy ashtray with both hands, when she asks me why I came back. The corners of her mouth are trembling, but she really wants to know why I left. In either case, it is the same, of course. I am unable to say right out.

"Couldn't I stay?" I ask. "Just for the day."

SHE MAKES THE WORLD FLAT

She is silent. The whole neighbourhood is silent and still (a pin could have been dropped in Norway or two doors down), until the hum of the fridge becomes a roar, the silence shattered.

My palms are sweating against the green glass.

"I could help Frank around the house," I say, facing my sister in her kitchen. "My plane doesn't leave until tomorrow."

She looks away, folding her lips into each other, holding them that way from the inside with her teeth. "It's late," she says.

"There's a lot of blue here," I say, pointing the ashtray toward the puzzle. "You said it yourself."

My sister is looking right at me. The lines between her eyes are deep and vertical. Before I'm aware of what's happened, I feel the ashtray deflect off my kneecap, and I hear it crash to the floor. My sister bites down on her lips and her eyes flinch.

"We can work together," I say, as a brittle shard crackles beneath my shoe.

She points to the kitchen table. "Don't forget your smokes," she says, then leads me from her kitchen. "Your nerves must be frayed worse than mine."

My sister opens the front door and kisses me on the cheek before I step onto her porch. The screen door closes behind me.

Across the street, the old man props a ladder against the first tree in his orchard, a short-bladed pruning saw in one hand, then he scrambles up among the limbs.

MY FINITE CHEVY

I DROVE TO THE PARK & Ride in I's '64 Chevy Belair, parked it beneath one of the tall lamps that helped illuminate the acres of asphalt, and then climbed aboard the city-bound bus. I sat in the usual seat, halfway down the aisle and on the same side as the doors.

As the bus pulled away from the curb it dawned on I that I was the first person on the bus. I had never been the very first person before. You was always sitting three seats behind I and fast asleep, which is why I found it an easy routine assuming the same seat each day.

I felt very uncomfortable as I wondered where You was and wondered if I was even sitting in the correct seat. I was used to a life of strict patterns and predictable events. You not sitting where You always sat threw I for an early morning

MY FINITE CHEVY

loop. Was You sick? Was You dead? Or had You just missed the bus?

No, You wouldn't have missed the bus. For three years I had driven I's Chevy to the same Park & Ride, got on the 323 and sat down three seats ahead of You. And You was always fast asleep: arms folded tightly over the breast of You's trench coat, the lapels buttoned beneath the folds of You's chin. You's hat was always tilted abruptly forward, covering You's forehead and eyes. I couldn't tell, even after three years, if You wore glasses.

The bus halted at the first stop, and I felt slightly more comfortable as I recognized a familiar You get on the bus. Not the first You, but a familiar You nonetheless. Day after day You wore the same brown tweed overcoat and the same black leather boots. It was the large mauve purse with the brass clasp that each day seemed out of place, but it too was always the same.

You looked toward I but didn't notice anything different, or really see I. You was busy arranging You's dress and purse to the comfortable position that would allow You to fall asleep during the long journey to town.

You was older than I (perhaps fifteen or twenty years older) and I understood that You's eyes weren't as accurate as I's, so it seemed logical for You not to notice that You wasn't sleeping three seats behind I.

The doors closed and the bus continued.

The next stop was You's: the young-businessman You with thick tawny hair that naturally repelled any form of precipitation. You always wore a smile and a wool suit (either baby or navy blue), but it was the dark blue and red argyle socks that each day distinguished You from all the others. You sat down across from You and glanced toward I, who was by this time beginning to fall asleep, preparing for the long journey into town. I began to nod off by the second stop and was fast asleep by the third, long before the bus completed its suburban stops and reached the freeway.

When I woke up, the bus was downtown, though not in motion. It was filled with Yous, some still asleep, others awake but drowsy, looking straight ahead to the front of the bus to where You was standing in the aisle. It was You who should have been sleeping three seats behind I. I recognized You at once by the tightly buttoned trench coat. You wore no eyeglasses.

This wasn't supposed to happen like this.

Was I dreaming?

Was You dreaming?

You's eyes peered from beneath the tilted hat, looking for something, someone. You's eyes opened wide as You unbuttoned then slipped a hand into You's breast pocket and pointed the other with outstretched finger at I and screamed, "You. YOU."

I removed I's glasses and rubbed the sleep from I's eyes. I's muscles tightened and pushed against the back support of the cushioned seat.

"I," I said, "I?" Then I stood and moved slowly into the aisle.

MY FINITE CHEVY

"You. You," You said, advancing down the aisle.

I stepped toward the rear of the bus, tripped over an umbrella handle, and fell backward.

You stood over I and produced from You's breast pocket a single fluorescent-red bus pass, which You held before I's eyes. In bold black lettering, it read: *Valid for three years.*

The look on You's face was confused, as was I's, but since You was leading, I would follow.

I took the bus pass and stood up, renewed.

Once on I's feet, You backed away, allowing I's safe return to a new seat, three behind where I had been sitting, and watched as You walked backward up the aisle and left the bus.

The bus pulled away but You on the sidewalk persisted in pointing and mouthing to I: "You. You."

I was confused as I watched. Then I whispered the word to I's self. "You. You?" and pointed to I.

You on the sidewalk read You's lips in the bus, lowered You's arm and outstretched forefinger, smiled, and walked away.

You fell asleep on the bus.

When You awoke, the bus was empty (except for You) and parked back at the Park & Ride depot in You's neighbourhood, just a few miles from where You lived. It was dark in the bus but even darker outside, so when You tried to look through the window all You could see was You's own reflection. Something was different, yet You couldn't say what that difference might be for sure. You was older, but that was only natural.

I CAN FIX ANYTHING

You scrambled across the aisle, crawled over the cushioned seats, and pressed You's face against the glass, searching the lot. Beneath a not-so-distant light sat a '64 Chevy, just where You had parked it so many times before.

A SITUATION COMEDY, NOW

MAYBERRY WAS WELL behind me as I drove, and Mount Pilot, I was almost sure, lay just beyond the next hill. The previous night, which I had observed from the steps of the gazebo in the centre of Mayberry, had gloated over its stars: their beauty in distant harmony was ticklish. A celebration throughout the sky. It was the kind of night that makes the world feel good all over, but tonight as I drove, as the distance grew between Mayberry and me, the sky was shallow, opaque, and its stars a solitary few.

Then suddenly, as I took my eyes from the road ahead, a star unpinned itself, toppled, and disappeared forever. In less time than it took me to gasp, a thought flashed before my headlights so quickly and passed with such force, that I was compelled to act instantly. My forward motion was stopped so suddenly and reversed so naturally that the exact point where my direction changed was a lone star that flashed and disappeared forever. The biggest and clearest decision of my life to this day is also the most mysterious. My home was north, but with the change in channels, an unexpected station break, I was headed south again, returning to Mayberry.

I had gone to Mayberry in the first place to either verify or dispel a rumour I had heard up north, but once there (Mayberry was always sunny) I had been taken in by the town's people, cradled at Sunday dinners, doted on, scripted into family picnics, until the rumour became unimportant, and I had left Mayberry (my first vacation in twenty years at an end) without knowing if the rumour were true or false.

There was little traffic on the highway as I headed toward town, and the small hours of the morning seemed the clearest. I'd be back in Mayberry just after dawn and the sun would be on my left.

I could have chosen, originally, to go to 211 Pine Street, Mayfield, U.S.A., and stay with the Cleavers. I could have shared a room with Wally and the Beaver, which would have been safe and secure. Or I could have gone out west to California (Beverly Hills, that is . . . swimming pools, movie stars) and stayed with Jed, Jethro, Ellie-May, and Granny, and that would have been a sound decision, but I had chosen Mayberry because I wanted to clear up the rumour once and for all that surrounded Floyd the barber. I used to wonder about Andy Taylor's wife: was she dead, or had she left him? No one ever mentioned anything about Mrs. Taylor. I wondered if she had died giving birth to Opie, and it was over this possibility that I too left the subject alone. Andy was a single father, and no one asked questions. Aunt Bee provided the motherly influence, so there was no question whether or not Opie was involved in a normal family environment.

Mayberry and I could live without Mrs. Taylor, but Floyd was the real mystery. I hadn't seen him on his feet in years. I remembered Floyd taking tickets at a dance, and once in a while he gave Andy or Howard a trim, but these events were only on the reruns, a long time ago when Opie was still cute and said funny things without knowing it. I was worried — Floyd was never on his feet, and for a barber that was strange. He often sat in the sun outside his shop, and on one occasion I saw him down at the diner having a coffee late one evening, after the episode in which Aunt Bee had grown a rose possessing such a unique colour-blend that everyone in town, including Clara (she and Aunt Bee were friendly competitors ever since Aunt Bee's triumph at the 1929 Miss America Pageant), had conceded first prize to Aunt Bee's *Snowdrop Spring* until Opie crippled the flower on the eve of the county fair with an errant football intended for the usually sure hands of his friend Billy. It all worked out when Opie remembered that his father had taken a picture of the rose before the break. Aunt Bee won the contest, and everyone celebrated down at the diner. Floyd was never far from the bench on the sidewalk in front of his shop. He loved to sit in the Mayberry sun.

❋

I sped along the interstate and adjusted my rear-view mirror. How many people are able to do this? To actually travel to a place, realize its perfection, and then to see so clearly a safe and secure home? My family was unimportant now, and I had no guilt about heading south, leaving them forever.

Perhaps I could get a job down at Mayberry City Hall working for Howard Sprague. He was kind to me when I had first come into town, and not only told me about Clara, who had a room to let, but walked me right to her doorstep and vouched for me. Who knows how long it would have taken to find room and board on my own? Howard even offered the spare room with him and his mother, the Widow Sprague, but of course I couldn't impose.

"No imposition," he said. Then he looked a bit bashful. "In fact, to tell you the truth, stranger, I'd enjoy the male company, another fella to pal around with, if you know what I mean."

"Thanks, Howard," I began to say.

"It's just me and my mother, you know?"

"I know what you mean," I said.

We stood on Clara's front porch. I had suspected he was a lonely man. His keys bounced between his fingers, inside his coat pocket.

"But I hear there's great fishing here in these parts. Small-mouth bass." I smiled at him and he looked down at his shoes.

"I bet you know all the best spots."

"Well . . ." He hesitated, then knocked quickly on Clara's front door. "Oh sure," he said, "oh sure I do, but to tell you the truth, I'm not much of a fisherman."

Before he could knock a second time, the drapes in the front-room window parted and fell together again at their seam. The hall light startled me.

"But we'll get together for sure, Howard," I said. "At Floyd's."

"Yes." Howard smiled. "At Floyd's," he said, and at that moment I really believed that Floyd was the reason I had come, though later I wondered if it had just been an excuse.

"I hope you like Clara," he said.

Clara, whom I remembered as being slightly heavier and not nearly as beautiful as she appeared before me that first night, was framed in the doorway. She smiled warmly and said, "Evening, Howard."

Clara and I had begun a friendship before Howard could formally introduce us. I watched our curiosity bloom into friendship and more, as she shook my hand and drew me in from her porch. Howard talked on about my character.

"Good evening, Howard," Clara called from over my shoulder as she closed the screen door with a delicate kick backward. She turned out the porch light, leaving Howard in the dark.

I CAN FIX ANYTHING

✦

I checked my fuel gauge. I had enough gas to get back to Mayberry, but I planned to top up the tank at Wally's Filling Station before heading into town. Goober was always good for a friendly chat, maybe a quick game of checkers.

The highway narrowed a bit as I came upon the older section of the interstate, and I slowed to forty. The sun was about to rise, and played tricks with the trees, so I had to watch for animals and obstacles on the road.

Soon I was driving into bright, sunny patches of light that stretched across the road like spaces between railway ties, then back into shadows. I imagined that each flash of sunlight through the forest was a complete day from sunrise to sundown, and as each day snapped by me a night followed just as quickly, from sundown to sunrise. I felt my life catching up with me. My past caught up with my future, or perhaps it had passed my future. At any rate, the precise point where my life had changed direction was lost forever and it didn't really matter. It was daylight as I approached the county line.

I rolled down the window and rested my arm against the outside of the door. The road began to straighten.

That first night in Mayberry, Clara drew me a bath that was so hot my whole body turned pink. She said it was the best thing after a long drive. "And you've certainly come a long way," she said. Then she left the bathroom door ajar, so that if I needed anything I could just yell. "I'll hear you calling," she said.

As it was, she spent most of the time carrying armfuls of linen up and down the hallway, so a whisper would have reached her. I very nearly fell asleep in the tub.

❂

The North Carolina miles rolled by faster than the years as I neared Mayberry. Birch and larch trees organized themselves on both sides of the interstate and crested on each foothill. Then they grew sparse and gave way to straight white fences and acres of pasture, collections of barns, stables, and farmhouses. Kids in overalls looked up from feeding their chickens and other morning chores, and waved when I honked the horn. A young farmer wiped his shirtsleeve across his forehead, then waved his hat in the air. The frayed straw along the brim fluttered in the southern breeze.

Again I felt these people and this place draw me, and again my reason for going to Mayberry seemed more like an excuse. It occurred to me that there was no reason to go to Mayberry other than to live there. I fooled myself into thinking that I could vacation in Mayberry whenever I wanted, but where's the commitment in that? My foot instantly weighed heavier on the accelerator.

If not with Howard down at City Hall, perhaps Helen Crump could get me on at the school, teaching part-time, or even doing janitorial work. That would give me evenings and late afternoons to jaw around the checkerboard with Andy and the fellas at Floyd's. Whatever job I did take would have to allow me hours on the bench in front of his shop. I could even work with Goober over at the filling station, I thought, but that would be a last resort. The filling station was on the outskirts and I wanted to be close to Floyd. Clara's place was perfect.

❂

Just a few more corners and a straight stretch or two between me and Goober, who would most likely be sitting by the gas pumps reading a comic book.

I slowed for a long lazy bend, then accelerated into the straightaway, but only slightly, because I recognized the billboard on the right and anticipated the highway patrolman who waited there. I was well under the speed limit, but as I passed the huge sign announcing the upcoming county fair, I checked my rear-view mirror again and saw the cruiser pull onto the road. A light was flashing. I immediately slowed, and as I eased onto the shoulder I wondered whether it was the same patrolman who had stopped me on my first trip into Mayberry. That officer hadn't given me a ticket, saying that the only reason he had stopped me was to ask if the car I drove was *one'a them Eur-o-pean jobbies*. He hadn't seen many of them, if any, in real life "Only on TV," he'd said.

I applied the emergency brake and got my licence from the glove compartment. The officer leaned in toward me, but I couldn't say if I recognized him or not. I didn't want to stare. The sunglasses, and the wooden match in his mouth, made him appear very confident, and that's important if people are going to feel safe and secure in his county. His mouth moved slowly around his chewing tobacco. He removed the matchstick from between his teeth.

"Woo-ee," he said, and spat a chaw toward the rear of my car that sounded like *pit-ding*. I imagined a long brown slug dripping from the centre of my rear hubcap. "This here one'a them Eu-or-pean jobbies?" He stuck the match between his teeth again and the sulphur tip pointed straight toward me.

"No, sir," I said. "It's from Detroit." I was about to jog his memory when I realized he was not the patrolman who had stopped me before. "It's newer than you've probably seen down here," I said.

He stared at me with that matchstick darting from side to side in front of my eyes, and for the first time since travelling south I felt intimidated, slightly threatened. It didn't last long, though, this feeling, because I knew (I was almost positive) there would be a happy ending. There's room for the odd snag, I thought, in a day that turns out well.

He took off his sunglasses and stood back for another look. He shook his head, laid a tar-coloured stain on the centre white line, and said, "Shee-oot, looks like somethin' twenty years outta the future, don't it, stranger?"

"Yes, it does," I said. "Was I speeding?" I was fairly certain I had been under the speed limit.

"Well no, I just wanted another look-see. You can pull on out." He squinted before he replaced his sunglasses and waved his arm to move me on. "You have a good day now, ya hear?"

"You too," I said, and pulled back onto the highway.

I CAN FIX ANYTHING

Even if I had been speeding, and even if he had given me a ticket, I'd have straightened it out in Mayberry. Barney told me he'd take care of any problem I had with the law.

"As long as it ain't of the serious nature, mind you," he said, as he tucked his thumbs into his belt and rocked back on his heels. "Law ain't here to dump on no strangers less'n them strangers turn out to be a member of the criminal element. Then there's me, the law"—he patted his revolver handle—"and baby makes three." His head nodded with his own words and he breathed in deeply. "Ain't that right, Ange?"

Andy looked up from his game of checkers when it became Opie's move, and began to smile. "Sure, Barn. You wanna finish sweep'n' those cells when you're done put'n' the fear of the law into this here stranger?"

I smiled at Andy's private joke, suspecting what was about to happen, as did everyone, excepting Barney Fife, that is. I had seen this happen before, and only Andy could pull it off better than if both parts were scripted. The initial clue: Andy's smile.

The first time Andy smiled in my direction, I remembered clearly, I could see that everything would work itself out within the half-hour. That was the way things happened in this town, and this town loved their sheriff, because Andy always did the right thing. The time when the lonely old travelling shoe salesman, who hadn't sold a single shoe in six months, came into town. Andy was the first one to go to the hotel room and lighten that salesman's soul, and of course the rest of Mayberry followed. They all bought shoes. In another episode, a few years back, a flimflam man blew into town claiming his partner was the direct descendant of Wyatt Earp, and together they staged a Wild West show the likes of this town had never seen. But Andy was suspicious from the very start, and he didn't hide it. So Clarence Earp challenged Andy to a showdown in Main Street, but when high noon rolled around, Andy wore no gun. He never wore a gun. Instead, he confronted Clarence with a sincere look in his eyes and a smile that could change the face of the world. Andy told him he didn't have to hide behind that guise. Young Clarence heard that it wasn't the Wild West any more (contrary to what his partner told him), and that he didn't have to go around this great country arm wrestling, or duelling, for people to like and respect him. "You can be Wendal, and people will respect you for that, if you let them," said Andy, and then he turned to the flimflam man and said, "And you don't have to listen to guys who want to turn a fast buck when they tell you you're somebody you're not."

Andy smiled, and the whole town warmed a few degrees. He had freed this young, confused stranger and shown him to himself. It wasn't only the smile, though, it was also the warmth and sincerity in the way he encountered folks. The sun appeared when Andy Taylor smiled on a situation. And the first time he smiled in my direction, he shook my hand.

"Glad to make your acquaintance, stranger. I hear y'all stayin' over at Clara's," Andy said. "Your move, Ope."

I CAN FIX ANYTHING

Opie moved his checker as Barney took the broom into the cell and began sweeping. He was mumbling about the actual length of the long arm of the law when the cell door closed, locking him up. He dropped the broom, turned quickly, and clenched his teeth. He was suddenly seething. His eyes narrowed, but he couldn't speak.

The smile widened across Andy's face, but Opie was still puzzled.

"Paw?"

"Yeah, Ope?"

"Why's Barney keep lockin' his-self up like that?"

"Well, Ope, ya see those keys a-hangin' on yonder wall?"

"Yeah, Paw."

"I a-spect Barney wants to test just how long the long arm of the law really is."

Barney moved to the front corner of the cell. He pressed his body sideways against the bars and reached out his arm.

"Don't look long enough, Paw."

"No, it don't, Ope. Best run over there and give the long arm a little hand."

"Okay, Paw."

Opie took the keys from the wall and released Barney. Everyone except Barney was laughing as he stormed out of the office.

But outside, sure enough, the sun was shining.

Mayberry, 1962, was the time and place for me.

✲

A SITUATION COMEDY, NOW

I pulled into the filling station. Goober recognized my car immediately, but he didn't approach me, or come near the pumps.

"Hey, stranger," he said.

"Hey, Goober." I got out of my car. "Bet you never thought you'd see me again." I held out my hand, but Goober didn't shake it. Instead, he pulled a rag from his back pocket and wiped his hands.

"That'a fact?" There was a sharp edge in Goober's voice. He looked toward the sky. His eyes were cloudy.

"To tell you the truth, Goob, I thought I'd settle down in Mayberry."

Goober stuffed the rag into his back pocket. "Mayberry ain't for you, stranger."

I didn't understand what was happening. Had I made a mistake by not returning north? Had I misinterpreted their sincerity when they all asked me to come back real soon? "And come back as often as you like," they had said. Was it something they did just to be polite to everyone who passed through their town, never expecting to be taken seriously? I stood quietly listening to a distant rumble echo over the foothills somewhere off behind me, and I thought of my family. It was a thought I had never had in quite the same way before. I wondered whether they were safe in a basic, fundamental way. Were they safe during winter? Would they be safe if the power went off? Would they be safe if a nuclear warhead dropped from the sky? Were they safe, and did they feel safe all the time?

I stared straight at Goober, and then I nodded. He shook his head.

"T'ain't no gas for you in these here pumps, stranger."

It seemed only the shell of Goober. The Goober I knew was friendly and naïve. I had laughed with Goober less than twenty-four hours earlier. This wasn't the same Goober.

I climbed back into my car and drove off toward Mayberry. I had friends there. Clara had promised to save my room. The second-best room in the house. "It's all that southern exposure and the morning sun," she had said.

The trees were taller for some reason as I neared town, and they stood closer to the road. I rolled up my window and checked my fuel gauge again. A wind began rustling branches and blew the odd scrap of paper across the highway. I closed my sunroof. Shadows disappeared altogether when the clouds moved in. As I passed the sign welcoming me to Mayberry, a few drops of rain sprinkled my windshield. I found myself driving with one foot on the brake. Dark branches climbed right across the road, not so high above me. Headlights appeared in my rear-view mirror and a horn sounded. I wanted to pull over but there was no shoulder. The flora was thick right to the road. The old pick-up truck swerved into the other lane, honked twice more, then rushed by me. I couldn't remember this stretch of road from my first trip, but it hadn't rained then. Everything looks different in the rain. When I reached the end of the tunnel (it was more like a long, grey-green tube), and the pick-up was a frantic cloud in the distance speeding off toward Mayberry, I noticed that the rain was not just falling but pouring, emptying the sky of all its colour. I had instinctively switched my wipers to a faster speed.

By the time I parked in front of Sheriff Taylor's office, the sky had dumped several inches of rain on the streets of Mayberry. The town was black and white in memory, but as I shifted across the front seat of my car and got out from the passenger side, the whole town huddled in greyness. A single bolt of lightning illuminated Main Street — fleeting shadows darted across the pavement — then a crash of thunder turned the whole town an even darker grey. I imagined the entire south grey and flooding, and it seemed to me then, as the cold water soaked into my skin, that Mayberry might not be the place nor the time to settle.

There, on the doorstep of the sheriff's office, a few short yards from the bench out front of Floyd's, I thought again of my family, though I could not picture them. Were they dry just then? And warm? But that was as far as I considered, because I wanted to think only of myself, my safety, and I was neither warm, nor was I dry. It was pointless to think of them now. Even if I had enough gas, the rain told me over and over that I couldn't leave, so I ducked into Andy's office.

Everyone was there, in out of the rain. Opie and Andy were playing checkers and eating fried chicken wings between moves. Aunt Bee and Clara were sitting in the corner by the rifle rack, silently knitting. A toilet flushed, a door opened,

I CAN FIX ANYTHING

and Otis staggered back to his cell. Barney locked the door, hung the keys on the wall, and cast a defensive stare over the room. Opie had his father down to his last three checkers, and by the look on Andy's face, he probably hadn't smiled all morning. Helen Crump marked papers at the desk beside Aunt Bee and Clara. Howard Sprague was smiling with his mother over tea in the other cell. Goober dangled his legs from atop Andy's desk, a small puddle of muddy water growing on the floor beneath his shoes. He was reading a Marvel comic book. Barney read over his shoulder and poked him in the ribs when he flipped the page too soon. Otis rolled onto his back and began snoring. Thunder rattled the town. Aunt Bee pulled a photograph of her prize-winning rose from her purse and passed it to Clara, who pressed her lips together. Emmett sat in the centre of the floor with tools and toaster parts spread around him in a loose circle. No one saw me, or showed any sign that they knew I was in the same room. Andy tried to concentrate on the checkers before him, but his thoughts were not on the game. There were lines on his forehead I had never seen before. He cleared his throat a few times and scratched his nose. His shoulders were narrow, not nearly as broad as I had remembered. He was deciding what to do, but I knew from the faint whistle I heard blowing in from the background, which concluded each episode, that there wasn't much time. Everyone waited for Andy Taylor's next move.

I felt like a stranger in my own home town.

The rain pounded against the window panes, a bolt of

A SITUATION COMEDY, NOW

lightning squeezed a flash between the blinds, a roll of thunder crashed down Main Street, a puddle formed around my feet, but nobody would look at me.

I had to do something. "Where's Floyd?" I inquired. "Isn't Floyd the barber here?"

They kept on reading (or just looking at the pictures), or knitting, or snoring, or marking, or fixing, or drinking tea and smiling and waiting for the sun to come out. All except Opie, who was still quite young. He looked up from the checkerboard in a familiar way. "Paw?" he asked.

"Yeah, Ope." It was Andy's move, but he wasn't concentrating on the game.

Opie gestured toward me. "You gonna make the stranger a reg'lar here in Mayberry, Paw?" he asked.

"Don't rightly know, Ope."

"How come he came back?"

Barney jabbed at Goober's ribs and Emmett dropped a screwdriver.

"I a-spect," said Andy, "it could be Clara's apple pie that brought him back."

Clara smiled without parting her lips or dropping a stitch, and nodded to Aunt Bee, who nodded in return.

"Or, could be he wants to work with Howard down at . . ."

Howard stood at the mention of his name, but his mother stopped him with a gentle hand on his forearm before he could leave the cell. "Gosh, Andy, it's a bit slow down at City Hall."

Emmett's toaster wouldn't pop, but he gave a laugh

I CAN FIX ANYTHING

anyway, and said, "I'd drive all the way from Mount Pilot for a slice'a Clara's pie."

"Apple pie," said Clara, and Aunt Bee chuckled. Everyone laughed except Andy and Otis, who was snoring in the cell. Helen put away her red pen and slipped the papers into her briefcase.

"Or," continued Andy, "could be he wants a job teachin' you youngsters."

"All done," said Helen. "Look, everyone. The rain's let up."

Everyone glanced through the windows, between the blinds.

"Where's Floyd?" I asked, but no one seemed to hear. "Is Floyd all right?" I was worried about Floyd. Where could he be in this rain?

"Or, Barney figures our stranger here is part'a the criminal element."

"He don't look like no criminal, Paw," said Opie, as he wiped his hands on his pants.

"That's the worst kind." Barney stood up and began rocking on his heels. "Ain't that right, Ange?"

Then Andy saw something he hadn't seen before, and suddenly moved a hand toward the checkerboard. He jumped three of Opie's checkers and received his crown. His smile began to grow again, and before anyone noticed it had filled the whole room, and then the town.

Long shadows formed across the floor between the narrow ribbons of sunlight that dashed in through the windows. The step dried around my feet.

A SITUATION COMEDY, NOW

Howard stood up quickly, before his mother could intercept him. "Hey, what about Floyd's?" he asked.

Emmett gathered the extra pieces into a pile. Andy had his son's last checker cornered with his king. Goober rolled his comic and stuffed it into his back pocket. Barney rocked forward onto the balls of his feet and then walked towards the cells. Otis was still snoring as Barney picked up his broom and began sweeping. Helen turned to Andy and said, "See you tonight, Andy. Same time?"

"'Bout eight o'clock."

"Bye-bye," said Helen.

Everyone said goodbye to Helen, and she smiled at me as she left the office.

Aunt Bee and Clara put away their knitting and walked up to me. Clara gently clasped my hand. "Your room's all ready. I'll bet you'd like a hot bath this evening."

"And dinner with us on Sunday," added Aunt Bee. "I won't hear 'no' for an answer."

The two women smiled courteously to one another as they walked toward the door.

The Widow Sprague led Howard past me. "I'll see you later at Floyd's," he whispered from the corner of his mouth. "Just taking my mother home." He winked.

"Come along, Howard," said his mother. "Have a nice day, stranger."

I winked back at Howard and smiled at his mother.

"I wouldn't mind taking up fishin' sometime," I heard Howard say from the sidewalk.

I CAN FIX ANYTHING

"See ya, Paw," said Opie, as he raced by me and hopped onto his waiting bicycle. "See ya, stranger," he called. The spokes twinkled in the sun. I waved after him.

Goober, Emmett, and Barney stood around me. Andy put his arm around my shoulders. His grip was firm. The checkerboard was tucked under his other arm.

Goober was excited. He bounced from foot to foot. "Let's go to Floyd's," he said.

We all left the office, Barney leading the way with three long strides. He sat down on the bench, which had dried completely in the short time since the downpour, and crossed his legs.

"It's gonna be another beautiful day," he said.

Emmett set his toaster and its extra parts on the sidewalk and sat down beside Barney. Goober took the checkerboard from Andy and pulled a chair out from the sheltered entrance to the barbershop.

Andy patted me before taking his arm away, and then he pointed to my car. "You best go get settled over at Clara's. We're fix'n' to set awhile at Floyd's." I felt his broad, open palm between my shoulder blades, as he patted my back again to start me walking. Everyone gave me a hearty, sincere smile, but it was Andy's that I felt warm my chilly bones. "Don't be a stranger now, ya hear?"

✪

Now I sit in my room at Clara's, the sun still pouring in from the south. From down the hall, I hear the bathtub filling. I'm

A SITUATION COMEDY, NOW

about to get up from my desk and go down to Floyd's, but Clara is drawing me the bath she promised before I leave, and there's a soft, parting whistle settling like stardust over the whole town. It lasts just about as long as a town clock chiming nine p.m., then fades away into silent darkness.

AT THE TURN OF THE CENTURY

He could not have said for certain how long he had been asleep, though *Thursday* stood out in his memory. He awoke in his small bedroom, in the apartment in which he lived alone with his mother and father. The young man rolled from his bed, feeling the sleepy numbness linger a moment, then drain from his limbs altogether. He assumed he would catch an appropriate bus, take a seat in the rear, and sit quietly re-reading the remaining pages of the book he had borrowed from his high school library, knowing full well the hero was indeed a cockroach and would not survive that condition.

Yes, it was Thursday.

AT THE TURN OF THE CENTURY

When he found himself on the sidewalk, retreating from the double doors of the bus instead of entering, the young man realized he was mistaken to assume anything. So instead, he began walking toward downtown.

A few buses passed him. Several more cars and countless more people passed him before he became aware that he was standing on a corner near the centre of town, gazing across the intersection at an all-night restaurant kitty-corner from the movie theatre in front of which he stood. He closed his eyes.

The young man had begun walking in a kind of sleep several months ago, just as he was finishing public school. At that time he convinced his mother he wasn't learning enough about the important things in life, like how to function efficiently in his urban environment, how to negotiate traffic, and where to go and what to do. There was too little time for sleep. There was not enough time for walking through the city, and there was no time at all for high school.

He quit school to catch up on his sleep. He now slept throughout the day, and walked most of the night, which caused his days and nights to eventually run together, their beginnings and endings open-ended. However, on occasion his mind was clearer, as was the case when he climbed into his bed early this morning and heard his mother search for her missing bowling shoe, when he concluded that it must be Thursday: bowling in the morning, then a six-hour shift in the shoe department of Sears throughout the afternoon. The month, however, remained a mystery.

"I have five minutes," his mother remarked matter-of-factly from the hall outside his bedroom.

The young man thought about how he noticed, only recently but with increased frequency, the method by which his mother had divided her life into five-minute intervals. There were five minutes preceding all events, there were five minutes between events, and there were, eventually, five minutes left in each event.

Then he thought about how disorganized his life had become, how the days ran together, how the months had vanished, and how the parts of each day dangled as if the master links which held the morning to the afternoon at one end, and the evening to the night at the other end, had worn out and simply fallen away.

In his bed, he heard his mother in the hall outside his door zip her other bowling shoe into her leather satchel. A closet door closed, and he pulled the cover over his head, shutting out the thinnest Thursday light.

The young man was already breathing in a slow, even rhythm when she called from the hallway, "Good morning, Gregory," and then "Good night," and he slept soundly all day until late in the afternoon or early into the evening, when he woke to find himself across the intersection from the all-night restaurant in the centre of town.

✪

AT THE TURN OF THE CENTURY

As dusk covered the city, falling around the shoulders of the young man as he stood on the street corner, a thousand tiny lights ignited along double tightropes into the four directions farther than he could see. Never before had he witnessed the streetlights coming to life, and he thought how fortunate he was to be standing where he was when he was, for the series of tiny slow-motion explosions had begun from this particular intersection and stretched all the way to the stars.

He faced the intersection, which he felt must be the centre of something very large and important, and considered finding a table in the all-night restaurant and completing the remaining fifteen pages of his book, when a woman with a huge metallic purse suddenly pushed past him to receive shelter beneath the theatre's illuminated awning. The young man put a hand against his stomach (perhaps he should've eaten at home) and noticed that it had begun to rain. He proceeded to cross the intersecting streets, obeying faithfully the green and red traffic lights.

He was thinking of Gregor Samsa when he was shown to a table on the upper level of the restaurant. The restaurant was crowded and smelled of many foods, but no one food could he identify. He ordered French fries with extra gravy, a small milk, and a cup of black tea, and then resumed dreaming of Kafka's hero waking from a sound sleep to find himself metamorphosed: transformed into a huge brown insect.

"But why a cockroach?" he said aloud. The hostess, who was passing by with a pot of coffee, paused in the aisle.

I CAN FIX ANYTHING

"More coffee?" she asked.

The waiter who had taken his order set down a small glass of milk, a silver pot of tea, and a plain brown mug. There was confusion with reference to which beverage the young patron had ordered. The waiter consulted his order pad. His face was Scandinavian-fair, and the young man with Kafka moving around his brain watched it redden.

"I believe he ordered tea," said the waiter at last.

"Did you order tea?" asked the hostess, who loomed over him with her coffee pot.

The young man moved farther into his booth.

"Yes. Tea," he said nervously.

"But didn't you just ask for coffee?"

"No. I said *cockroach*," said the young man in the booth, and he gave a quick smile to the waiter. "I ordered tea."

The hostess looked at them both, pressed her lips into what may or may not have been a smile, then rushed off to the lower level of the restaurant. The waiter left in the opposite direction, and the young man in the booth closed his eyes for a moment. Perhaps if he had said *dung-beetle* the confusion regarding his beverage might have been avoided.

Prior to this Thursday, the young man had gained confidence in himself when leaving the apartment. However, he continued to push doors when, at times, a pull was necessary, and he frequently went into a room for a specific purpose, and once there forgot what that purpose was. At times he would catch a distorted reflection of himself from the kettle, or a dent in the toaster, and in that instant he would forget. Consequently, he ate out more and more, mainly at late-night restaurants, discovering hunger at odd hours. But it had been days, perhaps weeks, since he had tripped over the coffee table or knocked his mother's food processor from the kitchen counter, which inevitably would attract his father's attention as he stared over his evening meal at the dining room table in preparation for the late shift at the mill.

"Gregory, is that you?" Mr. Sampson would pause for a moment, gather his concentration, then begin to eat again. Only on one occasion did the young man startle his father to the degree that he seized the nearest item, which happened to be an Macintosh apple, from the fruit bowl, and hurled it in the direction of the disturbance. The projectile struck Gregory squarely in the back. A bruise formed and still throbbed when the weather was damp and cold.

The young man removed his tea bag and poured from the little silver pot. He had without a doubt ordered tea.

Throughout the story, he thought almost out loud (for the thought moved his lips), you hoped that Gregor was dreaming, merely dreaming that he was a huge brown insect and that he would wake up at any moment to find himself still a young man, but somehow you knew he wouldn't wake up. He was already awake. Something in the narrator's tone told you that it was not a dream. Gregor Samsa was a cockroach.

The waiter brought the plate of French fries covered in thick brown gravy. The young man selected the larger of the two forks and dug into his fries. They were tough and took more than a reasonable amount of force to spear. They tasted fine, but their texture was suspect. The young man reasoned that because it was getting later in the evening, and because he was only moderately hungry, the fries only seemed tough, only seemed to be tougher than usual.

That's what it must have been like to live in Prague at the turn of the century, he thought, as he stuffed several fries into his mouth. Life was uncertain then. You were never really sure if you were awake or not, dreaming or not. You kept thinking that perhaps you were dreaming, and kept hoping that you would wake up to find yourself unchanged, everything unchanged, so you could continue doing what you had done before.

He scooped more fries into his mouth and chewed them slowly. He could not help but chew them slowly. The fries were very tough. They resisted the tines of his fork, but he was determined even if he wasn't all that hungry. He sipped his milk, and thin brown trails floated in arcs and swirled from the rim where his lips had touched the glass. He continued eating his fries and thinking.

But you never did wake up to find you were still the same person and that the world was the same world. And all the time you were believing that you and the world were just as before, and that at any moment you would wake up to continue as you had done before, something in the tone

AT THE TURN OF THE CENTURY

hinted the contrary, informed you of the contrary.

Only a few fries remained in a smeared pool of too much gravy and the young man chose the largest, which sat in the centre, to be his last. He poked it with his fork, but the fry refused to be penetrated, more so than its predecessors. The young man stabbed again, but the fry just rolled onto its side and settled comfortably into its gravy. It was in this position that it finally revealed itself. It was not a fry at all, but something only posing as a fry. It had a fingernail.

It was not a large finger, for it was slender and, despite being a good-sized fry, it was a rather small finger. It must be the little finger, but of which hand? thought the young man. As far as gender, it was impossible to say: either a prepubescent male or perhaps an adolescent female.

At that instant, on that particular thought, a dish crashed to the kitchen floor, and the young man fell from his booth and into the aisle.

Those in the restaurant suddenly woke up around the young man in the aisle, and for a very short time one minute directly followed the next so closely that everything began to happen at once. Many mouths spoke throughout mouthfuls of food, and twice as many hands reached and waved through the air above the tables, while ten times as many fingers articulated what the mouths were unable to say. Then all the voices settled down in a constant murmur around the young patron in the aisle, like a net so finely meshed it clung like a veil, and he noticed then that no one had taken notice. He rubbed his eyes, then dropped his hands to his sides.

The waiter and hostess flanked the young man who now stood quietly in front of his booth near the window. They looked at each other and there was, again, confusion. They looked to the young man, then to his plate. His novel lay on the red vinyl seat in the booth. He was reluctant to reach for it.

"I'll get the manager," said the hostess, and she disappeared around the corner into the kitchen. The waiter's face glowed a patchy, uneven red and he backed away. "She'll get the manager," he said.

The young man contemplated his vacant seat in the booth. The finger was very still on his plate and his hands were clenched inside his pockets. He hesitated a moment, decided not to venture after his book, knowing full well the hero and his family were doomed, then quietly slipped from the restaurant, past the cashier's desk and out onto the street.

The night air was cool against his eyelids (the rain had stopped), and he began walking in the way that seemed most familiar, alternating one foot forward, then the other, trying to remember if he had paid his bill or not.

I LOVE RAISINS

When we moved into our new home last spring, I looked forward to meeting interesting neighbours. Suburbs are full of neighbours and the concept of suburbs fascinated my wife and me: a careful grid of streets and avenues with countless houses (each with their own number) and very few vacant lots. The neighbourhood we chose was an established suburb with a fine past. Since we now had a residential lot in its future, the sun, I believed, would shine effortlessly over us and all our neighbours.

When we had lived in the city, joined to this suburb by a freeway, we'd take each other out on Sundays (sometimes I drove, other times my wife drove), and we pointed to houses we thought would make nice homes.

I CAN FIX ANYTHING

"Really, when you think about it," I said to my wife once, who was at the wheel, "any house would do."

"Yes," she said, "and even with some of these older houses, a little paint would brighten up the whole street."

So we put our names on the list and a year later, when we had moved to the top of that list, we were shown this house. We were standing on the narrow front porch when I asked the real estate agent a very important question.

"Oh yes," he said, and adjusted the lapel of his gold blazer. "These houses are full of neighbours."

But we've managed to meet only one set of neighbours so far: an ex-railwayman named Billy Simington and his wife, Ethel, whose names I forgot three minutes after our introductions, referring to them as Bob and Mabel (as if I could be blamed).

This morning, I spotted him on his front porch. I politely yelled, "Oh, Bob, have you got a 9/16 wrench I could borrow with which I can repair my underground-sprinkler system?" He didn't respond at first, just looked to his wife, who was seated in a wheelchair beside him there on the porch "Yes, uh . . . John, you can come over and borrow it if you like, John," he finally said. "It's in my basement, but I'd rather not leave my wife just yet here on the porch. You understand."

His porch was recently painted and he leaned over the white railing. I looked aimlessly around my front porch feeling slightly embarrassed for him, not because of his wife, and not because our porch was in need of paint, but because my name is Phil (actually Phillip). But, not wanting to shut out possible relations with my only neighbour thus far, I left my porch and walked toward his basement door with as little hesitation as humanly possible, since he obviously believed that by calling me John the odds were with him. John is such a common name, and I wanted to give him the benefit of his doubts by not correcting him at that moment, but at the same time I felt that if he were a neighbour who really cared about being a neighbour like my wife and I did, he would have realized that in the year of my birth—a quick estimation as to my year of birth would have done it—John was not the popular name it is today, not the name given most often by parents to their infant sons. Rather, it was James, which of course is not my name either, but nonetheless would have sat better with me.

"Phil." My wife leaned out the bedroom window on the third floor. She used the spare room as her studio. She had set up her easel, and worked daily on a landscape of the view from that window. "Where are you off to?" she asked, just as I reached our property line.

"Over to Bob's." I shielded the sun from my eyes as I looked up to her. "He has a 9/16 in his basement," I said, which in retrospect must have seemed ironic to her and a bit confusing, since I was a journeyman plumber and the only person on our street with an underground-sprinkler system, which I installed before re-landscaping, and there I was leaving our home on a quest for some sort of wrench of which I must have had plenty, and going to Bob's whose name she

I CAN FIX ANYTHING

knew to be Billy. She may have believed I had met other neighbours besides the ex-railwayman and his wife, which accounted for the smile that began to grow across her face, no doubt remembering the countless hours she had spent consoling me in that very room from which she called because I had not met the interesting neighbours for whom I longed.

"Have a nice time," she said with a huge smile that filled the window pane. "Don't be long. Remember, you have muffins in the oven."

"Yes, muffins. I won't forget," I said, but I fantasized about exchanging lawn-fertilizing techniques next spring and offering to clear the snow from Bob and Mabel's walk during the upcoming winter. The leaves will be falling soon and they'll need raking.

"That's one fine irrigation system you've got there," Bob said as I approached. His Adam's apple jumps when he laughs.

"Thanks, Bobby." I smiled up at him and he smiled in return. I felt we were quickly becoming not just neighbours but good neighbours, and that we were both headed for this common goal. Perhaps next spring we could build a fence together.

"And how are you today, Mabel?" Mabel's wheelchair was facing away from me, so I couldn't see her face. I smiled even more warmly at Bob on his porch to compensate for Mabel not being able to see me, but I did not receive a reply.

Bob turned toward his wife and mumbled something.

I remained standing on the sidewalk, a smile planted on

I LOVE RAISINS

my face, just in case Mabel approached the railing. That's how I wanted her to see me.

"Fine, John, thank you." Mabel's voice hesitated around her greeting, but I imagined her face with a smile. Of all the things harboured by neighbours in suburbs, suspicion is not among them.

I pointed to the door beneath the porch. "Through here, Bob?"

Bob tapped twice on the aluminum siding with his index finger, then pointed to my right. "Yes, John, and then to your right," he said.

The door closed behind me as I turned on the light and relaxed my face. Then a pang of anxiety that I couldn't ignore rushed over me, and I suddenly wondered if Bob and Mabel shared my desire for interesting neighbours. Were they happy? Would they have been happier if the house next to theirs had remained vacant forever? Surely neighbours should want other neighbours. It's the foundation on which suburbs are built. Had I moved into a house previously owned by neighbours with a reputation? Had Bob and Mabel counted the years, days, even hours until they could have peace without pesky neighbours who always borrowed items and never returned them? Did I really want to borrow this wrench? Was that why Bob hesitated before consenting to loan it? What did he say to his wife when I greeted them both so openly and so warmly from their front walk? Why did he turn from me? Was she the sceptic? Were they suspicious?

I stumbled over a bundle of newspapers and collapsed into

I CAN FIX ANYTHING

a stack of *Life* magazines across from Bob's workbench. Was this the place I had chosen to live? The life of a neighbour. My hands held the full weight of my head as I squirmed, trying to find my footing amid the pages of world events dating back to the years long before I was born.

A single light bulb swung above me, its light ricocheting from wall to wall. The corners filled with light then emptied. There was a lot of darkness. Three mannequins, with just five tangled arms among them, stared at the floor from their corner. Rows of jars containing nails, screws, nuts, and bolts, their lids fastened to the crossbeams of the basement ceiling, vanished like planets and reappeared like stars in the low, mysterious sky above me.

Then, not as quickly as my instincts had begged, I said, "Awwe-ugh."

There came, almost at once, three light taps from somewhere in the basement.

"Are you all right, Phil?" Bob knocked on the outside of his basement door.

It suddenly struck me. He did know my name, but had decided not to use it until now. What was he up to?

"Yes . . . ," I scrambled, beginning to panic, " . . . uh, did you say on my right or your left?" I jumped to my feet and gathered his stack of *Life* into a pile the best I could.

"Same thing, isn't it, Phil? Can I come in?"

He had used my name again to refer to me. What was he up to?

"Of course, Bob." I grabbed the first wrench I saw. "Your

basement." I stood in front of the bench examining the tool as Bob entered his basement. He raised his right hand and the light bulb was suddenly still.

"This should do the trick," I said. My knees were braced against the bench leg as I turned toward him.

"We were beginning to worry about you, Phil. My basement isn't that big."

I could only make out his silhouette as he stood in the doorway. Over his shoulder, our neighbourhood stretched farther than I could see, but right across the street a middle-aged neighbour removed two bright pink flamingos from her lawn, preparing to mow.

"That's a monkey wrench," said Bob.

"Yes." I leaned against the sturdy bench and straightened my legs.

Bob stepped from the doorway into the light of his basement. He took the monkey wrench from my hands, gave me an open-end 9/16, and led me through the door. I slipped the wrench into my back pocket.

We were greeted on the sidewalk by my wife.

"You were gone so long," she said. "Is it a big basement?"

"No," I told her, "but dark, even with the light." I wanted to hug her forever, bury my head in her warm hands, but instead I asked, "What's that you have there?"

"Your muffins, dear."

"My muffins," I said, but I really wanted to know how long had they been in the oven and were they burnt? How long had I been in Bob's basement?

"Golden brown," said my wife, who often read my mind. She handed me the muffin tin draped in a light blue tea towel. I received the muffins and turned to Bob.

"I baked these just for you and Mabel, Bob. I hope you like raisins as much as I do."

SUPPLY AND DEMAND

You arrive home a stroke on the other side of midnight—your shift has been a final bust—and change from your uniform into your favourite powder-blue pajamas. You mix yourself a liberal gin and tonic, and turn on the TV. This month's winning lottery numbers (none of which are yours) run across the bottom of the small screen, followed by a lengthy series of advertisements. You watch the first half of the Letterman show: the footage David shows is of brown shopping bags filled with fruit and vegetables soaring through the air in slow motion—all you see is blue sky around the bag. A few oranges topple away in flight, then the screen fills with concrete as bag meets sidewalk and the fresh produce paints a sudden, violent stain on a grey sidewalk somewhere in New York. Over and over

I CAN FIX ANYTHING

the film is shown, sometimes in fast motion, other times in slow, but each time the impact takes you by surprise, even when you see it coming.

When your glass is empty, you turn off the set and head for bed.

✽

You're slow to wake up Wednesday morning, but you soon realize the phone is ringing. You curl both pillows around your head and the ringing stops. What seems like a few moments later, you wake again, and this time your eyes open to the sound of someone rapping on your front door.

In your blue pajamas you stand holding open the front door. Two tapered young men, wide at the shoulders, narrow through the hips, each with a thick brown moustache, stand before you on the small concrete porch. Their uniforms are grey with a single dark blue stripe running down the outside of each pant-leg. You're distracted by a warm breeze blowing in from the street which smells remotely of chlorine. Your lips are dry. Birds sing.

A car horn breaks the neighbourhood morning, and both men turn in unison to face the car parked on the street in front of your house. METRO-TRANSIT is displayed in bold black letters on the passenger door. The door flings open and a woman gets out to stand on the curb. She too is in uniform.

Across the street, in the grey house with weathered storm-shutters, Mrs. Campbell stands in her front window. Her fists are on her hips, a stern look on her angular face. Whether it's in the mall, or at the bank, or even the one time when she rode your bus, whatever she sees you doing, she looks down upon you with disapproval. You've never spoken. Perhaps she does not disapprove of what it is you're doing; it's just as likely the way you're going about it that prompts her to frown and shake her head slowly from side to side, as she does now. She removes her eyeglasses, allowing them to hang from her neck on their fine gold chain. She's your neighbour, and you've never spoken.

The woman in uniform yells something then climbs back into the car, but you fail to understand, because you're distracted by the light breeze, the smell in the air, the birds, and Mrs. Campbell. The two men leave your porch. You have said nothing to them, but you understand that you are no longer a bus driver. Other than this, everything seems the way it has come to be.

The transit car makes a u-turn on the wide street and zooms away. Mrs Campbell disappears into her house. You have a strong sense that she could never like you, though you've lived on opposite sides of the same street for years.

You leave your front door open to catch some of the breeze, and walk down the hall into the kitchen. You stare for a moment at the linoleum, the random gold fleck scattered across the flat red plane. Fixing yourself a special breakfast seems an appropriate way to begin the day.

In the late afternoon you leave the kitchen through the

I CAN FIX ANYTHING

laundry room and enter your garage. You pull open the big aluminum door, then climb into your car and back out onto the driveway. You leave the motor running while you get out and close the garage door, all in all a bothersome procedure, but there's no way around it. You back onto your street and drive into town, to the Holiday Inn.

You walk up the steps and into the lobby. Ahead of you a sign beckons: the paveway road to success. Inside, in the Diamond Soirée and Convention Room, beneath the twin chandeliers, clusters of people are scattered about, mostly groups of twos or threes, listening attentively to the person among them who wears the bright red blazer with gold trim, each with a name-tag on the lapel. The room hums with voices (creating a strange and haunting harmony) and you are the only recruit not drinking from a styrofoam cup, nor eating doughnuts wrapped in small white napkins.

At your right you feel something warm against your elbow. A young woman rests her fingertips on your forearm. Her hair is long and straight with many shades of red running through it; her eyes are a rare chestnut. She guides you across the room towards the cloth-covered tables, and then disappears into the crowd.

You're about to bite into a jelly doughnut, already anticipating the layers of sugared pastry, the suddenness of the jelly, when suddenly you spot a short, pudgy man standing on the other side of the coffee urn. Is it true the shorter a man is the balder he can be? He has spotted you. He wears a red blazer with gold trim and his name is Chester.

SUPPLY AND DEMAND

"You're new here," he says. "I saw you come in." He sweeps his hands to one side and indicates a clear path through the crowd. "I'll come round." He extends his right hand and moves swiftly around the table. You set your coffee down next to the tray of doughnuts and prepare to meet him. "We all come round," he says, standing before you, shaking your hand enthusiastically. His face is red and he wears a crewcut like a helmet. He rests his left hand upon your shoulder like an old friend. "Success," he whispers. "No, don't say anything yet." He leans forward on his toes, then rocks back on his heels. He reaches into his breast pocket and produces a wafer-thin object. "They're our finest item." He tilts his head back, checking your eyes to make sure he has your attention. "All you need do is take this sample calculator, go round explaining to customers—your neighbours, relations, friends from work, et cetera"—he places the unit delicately in your open hand—"how much easier their lives become with one of these in their pocket, or purse." Chester points to the tiny object—weighing no more than a single playing card—resting in the palm of your hand, then winks.

You try to remember the last time anybody winked at you.

"They sell themselves, really," he says.

The Paveway Pocket Calculator feels like an after-dinner mint melting in your open right hand.

The informational video, "Pave Your Road," makes perfect sense. As long as there is a demand, a supply is required. Create a demand that you are able to supply. That part of the video made absolute sense. But there was nothing in it specifically defining the course of action for the object lying in your hand.

❂

After the show Chester leads you to a smaller room, where you're invited to sign the official papers and receive brochures and instruction booklets. Then he walks you through the rear exit and out to your car. How did he know where you had parked?

The air is clean after last night's rain. A line of taxis inches forward in front of the bus station a few blocks down. The second 'n' in the Holiday Inn sign is burnt out, but the rest of the city shines in your eyes, just like new.

It's a warm evening so you roll open the driver's side window. You turn off the radio just as the street lamps begin to light. A warm front, which is unusual for this early in the year, is moving in from the west. Fog begins to form on the road and hovers in slow, rolling clouds over the asphalt. The road becomes a lone straight slab of dry ice. It's a warm spring evening and you're flying home with your window rolled down.

As you round the final corner and pull onto your street, you see Mr. Campbell levelling the top of the laurel hedge that runs between his front yard and the Balaclavas' next door. He shuts off the Black & Decker and sets it carefully on the lawn. His mouth is contorted in a half-grimace, half-smile as he eyes the tops of his laurels. A long orange cord runs in loops and circles across the front yard, up the steps,

SUPPLY AND DEMAND

and then disappears into the house through a narrow crack left by the open door. In your rear-view mirror, as you pull into your driveway, Mrs. Campbell appears in her front room window. Opening your garage door, you glance over your shoulder but she has disappeared. You tuck the Paveway Merchandising Kit under your arm and carry it into the kitchen.

Weeks pass without a sale. Before you, on the kitchen table, an order book, a mug of coffee, a telephone book, and the sample Paveway Pocket Calculator all sit waiting for your attention. The telephone book lays open at the B's, but you're already discouraged. You gather up the order book and a pen, finish the last cold sip of coffee, and take your Paveway Pocket Calculator to the streets of your neighbourhood.

Eleven doors later, you stop short of the Campbells' and decide to break for lunch. You descend the Balaclavas' stairs and cross their lawn, stepping around the flowerbeds.

The tiny calculator is melting in your palm. You pause on the curb near the end of the laurel hedge and regard your house in the near distance. You should have painted last spring, when you would have had help, and this fall, you should fertilize, aerate, and lime. A headache begins behind your eyes and builds towards your temples as you step from the curb and cross the street. You almost wish for a speeding motorist, perhaps someone who is not fully attentive. But then, how could you wish that on anyone?

I CAN FIX ANYTHING

❂

One then two months pass nearly all at once without a sale. Instead of the encouraging letters you have always received in the past from Paveway Sales Ltd., today's letter is threatening. Unless you finalize twenty sales within the next four weeks, your position with Paveway, along with the possession of the sample calculator, will be *renegotiated*.

You refold the paper and close it into the phone book. You stand up and wander around your kitchen. Again you sit. You lean forward to rest your head in your hands, and face the floor. You begin to see things in the simple gold fleck that you've never seen before: constellations, dot-to-dot cartoon characters, highways connecting cities you've never seen except on maps, faces of people you used to know, a detailed plan of a doghouse you never finished, a rough sketch of a garden shed you never even started. All this, and more.

The afternoon rushes through your kitchen, and just as the sun is beginning to sink, you mix yourself a gin with ice and a little tap water, and move into the living room. You sit down in your armchair and stare into the TV screen. You stare all evening, pausing only to refill your glass. Just past midnight you get up and turn on the set. You flip the dial to your local cable network and adjust the fine-tuning. A group of very familiar numbers march triumphantly across the screen of your fourteen-inch black-and-white.

You get up and walk to the kitchen where you check the numbers from the screen against those on the ticket taped to

SUPPLY AND DEMAND

your fridge. You head straight to your bedroom and crawl under the covers. The gin sends you quickly to asleep.

❂

The next day, once you've cashed the cheque and secured the majority of your funds in the credit union, you make a few quick purchases before leaving the mall and heading straight home. While climbing out of your car, you're suddenly struck by the modesty of your small three-bedroom house among all the others that line your street. You all began with virtually the same house, same design, and same plans. You fold your arms and lean against the car door. The side-view mirror presses against your hip. The wide streets, the uniformity of houses, garden plants, lawns, and shrubbery: you can't think of anywhere else you could live. You who now have the choice. A modest neighbourhood, though the Marshalls have had an electronic garage-door opener for months.

You climb back into your car and park in the garage. You carry the two canvas bags into the kitchen, along with the telephone answering machine tucked under an arm. Emptying the money on the table, you glance over your shoulder. The curtains are closed across the window above the kitchen sink. You'll need a secure yet accessible place to hide this cash. Somewhere discreet but close at hand. You remove the knives, forks, and spoons from the cutlery drawer and replace them with neat stacks of tens, twenties, and hundreds. What doesn't fit in the drawer next to the sink you return to the canvas bags and stow in the broom closet, behind the ironing board. You make yourself a pot of strong coffee and sit down at the kitchen table with a mug. You set to work hooking the answering machine into the telephone line so you won't have to be disturbed by incoming calls. You set the timing mechanism so the machine can record a three-minute message.

❁

While watching a rerun of *Happy Days* later in the afternoon, a plan begins to shape itself, much like the images that sprang from the gold fleck of your kitchen floor, but your concentration is interrupted by two men from Sears who deliver a La-Z-Boy recliner. You help by pushing your old armchair across the living room floor and into the far corner. You point to the spot where you want the La-Z-Boy to sit. Just as the two Sears men leave, two men from Furniture City arrive on your front walkway. They struggle with a huge wooden crate containing a 26-inch Zenith console model. You carry your old set into the corner and place it on an end-table in front of the old armchair. The TV and chair form a monument to how your life used to be.

Later, reclined before this week's edition of *Venture* with a Tom Collins in hand, you find that throughout the afternoon and early evening, your plan has returned and taken shape around you. Venture. Without working out all the kinks, you decide to re-create your life. It suddenly makes sense. Supply and demand. Success.

❁

SUPPLY AND DEMAND

The next morning you wake up ready to begin again. You head straight for the kitchen and sit at the table. You open your Paveway Official Order Book, complete fifty invoices, and sell fifty Paveway Pocket Calculators to yourself. Then you order more order books.

Over the next few weeks you establish a casual routine, working for an hour each morning (the remainder of your days are left free) filling out order forms at the kitchen table, continuing your way through the phone directory or, sometimes, creating the entire name, address, and phone number of the purchaser on your own.

You set company records for the months of August and September in both sales and merchandise delivery. Everything goes through you. You receive weekly bonuses and immediately invest the profits in Paveway Pocket Calculators.

❂

One morning after work, while sitting in your recliner watching a rerun of *The Beverly Hillbillies,* your phone suddenly rings. You follow the cord which leads you to the kitchen table. The last call you had was weeks ago and it had been the last in a fast-paced series of real estate agents, life insurance salespeople, a few inventors, and one young landscape painter. You wait for the tone, then the message begins.

It's a long distance call but there's little static, and the woman's voice at the distant end of the line is clear and delicately resonant. You fail to remember her name seconds after her introduction. She begins to enchant you with praise of your marketing skills and the most efficient rate of "follow-through and delivery" in the company's history. You listen, standing over the machine. She invites you to New York to conduct a Paveway Sales seminar with a title like "Filling the Need," or "Planting the Seed," but you're distracted by the melody in her voice, and the strange sounds echoing in your head.

Your palms moisten. You can check the details later on Playback.

She knows she has just thirty seconds remaining so she begins to speak more quickly.

Where in Paveway's World have you chosen to spend your all-expense paid vacation of lifetime?

Why not co-ordinate the trip with the dates of the Paveway Sales Conference in New York, and more precisely, with the date tentatively set for your seminar?

Get in touch with us as soon as possible, she prompts, then hangs up.

You sit down at the table, staring at the now-quiet phone, the machine beside it, and the flashing green light that signifies a message has been left. Go, go.

But you can't leave for New York or some tropical clime: your whole marketing strategy of supply and demand would collapse. You erase the message immediately; however, over the next few weeks, new messages are recorded, until finally you unplug the phone altogether.

SUPPLY AND DEMAND

✺

Late one afternoon, you're awakened by slamming car doors. You climb from your recliner and rush to the living room window. The sleep is still in your eyes, a bad taste in your mouth. Across the street, Mr. Campbell is unloading an aluminum ladder from the roof rack, and gallon buckets of paint from the back seat of his car. Mrs. Campbell, in the front window, indicates with her baby-finger for her husband to begin with the storm shutter to her right, nearest the front door.

You turn and walk slowly down the hallway, rubbing your eyes and face. You undress in the bathroom, shower, and slip into a clean pair of your powder-blue pajama bottoms. You comb your hair and brush your teeth, then return to the living room window. You part the curtains. Your neighbourhood has changed, though you can't tell, at a glance, in what way. But something tragic has fallen, again. Very suddenly.

An ambulance backs into the Campbells' driveway. Something has happened very quickly in a short period of time, and you missed it. Mrs. Campbell is not in her window; nor is Mr. Campbell on the ladder. A can of white paint hangs by its handle from a hook near the top rung. There is no sign of a paint brush, though half of one shutter is whiter than the other. Perhaps if you had spoken to the Campbells, said hello in the grocery store, or waved from your car, you would feel like going across the street to discover the details of what happened, but then, what could you do? Mrs. Balaclava from next door is watching from her front window, and the twins are circling the street on their mountain bikes in front of the Campbells' driveway, just a few metres from the front bumper of the ambulance. Mrs. Marshall appears from the right edge of your peripheral vision and walks in a diagonal across your lawn, past the boys on their bikes, and up the Campbells' front steps. The door opens a crack—it's dark inside—and Mrs. Marshall slips in. The boys stop cycling and wait at the curb while a stretcher is carried down the front steps, wheeled along the walkway, and loaded into the rear of the ambulance. The doors close with two solid thuds. It pauses at the end of the driveway next to the Balaclava twins, then pulls onto the road and disappears down the street, no lights and no sirens. You let the curtains fall closed and the living room becomes dark again.

✦

You've used your remote-controlled garage door twice: once to open it and once to close it up again. Your three-bedroom home has rapidly filled with Paveway Pocket Calculators. You've stacked boxes in the guest room, in the nursery, and in the closet of the master bedroom.

You're the top salesperson of the fiscal quarter, and you order more order books.

✦

On a mid-November morning, while you ride your John Deere around the front lawn for the final time this year, a

SUPPLY AND DEMAND

rented van pulls up alongside the curb in front of your house. You shift the Deere into neutral and sit forward over the steering wheel. From your opposite vantage points, Mrs. Campbell and you watch a film crew leap from the rear doors of the van and begin setting up. A man with a camera on his shoulder is directed by a woman holding a clipboard in one hand and a stopwatch in the other, to begin a wide pan of the neighbourhood. An establishing shot, she says. She wants the camera to complete the shot with a slow close-up of your front door. Mrs. Campbell watches for a brief moment, glances up and down her street, then disappears from her front window. The cameraman guides his lens around the neighbourhood and focuses first on your front door, then on the van. The passenger-side door opens and Morley Safer steps out and walks across your freshly mowed lawn, heading straight toward you with a black vinyl folder tucked under his right arm.

"You didn't return our calls," he says. "Then there was no answer, no phone, no nothing." A thin smile is the best he can do. "It made us very curious."

You shut off the motor and agree to a short interview, but only because you notice the glowing red lights atop the two cameras now flanking Morley, and you don't want to be one of those people who refuse an interview on *60 Minutes*, one of those who appear to have a secret they want kept. A third camera, much larger than the two hand-held ones, is unloaded from the van onto the sidewalk in front of your house. Mrs. Campbell has reappeared in her window, but she only watches for another moment, then she is gone. Where are the Balaclava twins, the Marshalls' girl? Isn't anybody interested in what's happening in their own neighbourhood?

Morley suggests the inside of your home as the setting for "the spot." The hub of your operation embodies the natural drama of your climb to the top.

Inside is out, as far as you're concerned, but anywhere from the front door to the street is just fine with you.

The first two questions are easy, and you answer each the same way: supply and demand, Mr. Safer, supply and demand.

Mr. Safer adjusts his stance, kicks at some grass cuttings that have stuck to the toes of his shoes. He launches into his next question, but you are distracted; something is about to happen at Mrs. Campbell's. "Certainly the foundations of the present economy, and the peripheral fixtures—the concept of supply and demand being one such fixture—are firmly established, and have been this way for a very, very long time. How can a person such as yourself, with little or no training in the field, an obscure and vague past, climb his way to the top of an extremely competitive market?"

You create new ways of saying supply and demand; sometimes you answer with demand and supply, but essentially it's supply and demand. You lean across the steering wheel of the small tractor. There is movement in the house across the street, in Mrs. Campbell's front curtains.

Mr. Safer is documenting several horror stories about people whose fortunes were swindled away by crafty salespeople, such

SUPPLY AND DEMAND

as yourself. Many of these stories were done on *60 Minutes,* he says. Millions of viewers watched in neighbourhoods much like this one. He makes a slow sweeping gesture with his empty hand indicating your neighbourhood. "I have a very strong hunch," he says, "many of your neighbours watched."

The director says everyone is ready to shoot the major transaction. Morley wishes to purchase a PPC.

A Paveway Pocket Calculator.

The script is: you're inside your house watching TV, taking some time off to relax and unwind, when a knock is heard at the front door. Mr. Safer stands on your front porch and makes his request. You step out on your porch, closing the door behind you. You have a Paveway Pocket Calculator in the single back pocket of your pajama bottoms. Mr. Safer hands over the money, and you begin to write him a receipt. The cameras tape it all, but as you fill in the appropriate information for the sale, and while Mr. Safer speaks to the cameras under the direction of the woman with the clipboard, you look up from your pad, over the little red lights and across the street.

This was not in the script: Mrs. Campbell folds her arms across her stomach and watches from a narrow part in the living room curtains as her front door swings open and Mr. Marshall emerges carrying an oak end-table. He places it on the lawn in front of the flower garden at the base of the steps. The twins appear and descend the steps with a heavy coffee table. They set it next to the end-table. They're followed by

I CAN FIX ANYTHING

Mr. Balaclava, who manages a dining room chair under each arm.

You make mental plans to check your local TV listings. One Sunday in the near future you'll watch your first sale, and it will be on national television with millions of viewers watching from neighbourhoods all over the continent. You sign the receipt and mark it *paid*.

Mrs. Campbell is unaware of you on your front porch. She seems unaware of all the TV cameras arranged on your front lawn. She puts a hand to her cheek, her head tilts to one side, while a lamp is set on the end-table and a matching pair of armchairs are placed before her, in front of the flower garden.

Mr. Safer turns to accept his receipt and to shake your hand. You smile and nod to the cameras.

A huge yellow and green moving truck pulls up and parks across the street, blocking the Campbells' house from your view.

The red lights go out and the crew quickly pack up their equipment. Mr. Safer climbs into the front passenger seat.

Two men in white overalls load furniture into the rear of the big yellow and green truck across the street.

You're standing on your front porch, waving goodbye to Morley and the crew. Once their rented van is out of sight, you walk to the kitchen, mix yourself a tall gin and tonic with a twist, and return to the living room and to your favourite chair. The TV is on, but the volume is low. Even though you cannot see them, you're distracted by the two men in white, loading Mrs. Campbell's belongings into the back of their

SUPPLY AND DEMAND

truck. You get up from your chair to stand for a moment before your front room window. In an hour or two the house across the street will be empty. You can see it coming, but it will take you by surprise the next time you look. You close the curtains so no light at all can enter, and return to your recliner.

NAKED US

Later that same day, Emma would undergo the first official test of her young life at the community pool, while I would administer the first mid-term of my young teaching career up at the university. Anxiety occupied us both, while Lois offered balance and perspective. The October sun warmed our evenly-tanned bodies as we naked three stood on the small front porch of our modest new home. I glanced up one side of our street, then down the other; the rows of neatly painted houses much like our own, the trimmed lawns, hedges of laurel and young fir. There was a third factor, however, which at the time I thought unrelated. My morning erection, the one with which I had awakened,, had not yet subsided, and as a consequence, occupied a modest orbital space in the centre of our family triangle. Otherwise, all seemed as it should be.

I set my briefcase on the welcome mat and knelt to wish Emma success. I wore only my favorite argyle socks, my brown brogues, and the engraved wrist watch Lo had given me on our fifth anniversary. Anything else would have been too much, too contrived, and I clearly did not want to unnerve my students with abnormal behavior. I always carried my briefcase.

"Good luck, Daddy," said Emma, lightly tapping my shoulder. She's blonde and beautiful with a dimple in her chin, just like her mother. She also has her mother's casual confidence, her ease and co-ordination, even though she is small for five-and-a-half, and not a strong child physically.

"And good luck to you, too," I said, and kissed her forehead. Emma was going for her Floater's Badge at the community pool that afternoon, yet she had not forgotten that I wanted my students to do well. I wanted so much for her to float.

The sun was still low in the sky, creating a warm blanket over my back as I kissed Lois, who stood next to Emma in the open doorway. She rested a hand on my right hip, then nodded. Lois can be extremely subtle.

"I thought we took care of that," she said, indicating my obvious anxiety, and I could see in the dimples that began to form in her cheeks that she wanted to smile—maybe even laugh out loud—but she held back, not wanting Emma to discover that something might be awry. That things may not be progressing in their usual manner.

Emma's hair is fine, and cut short over her tiny head, like a swimming cap. She loves the water. She squinted up at us, glancing from one to the other. She'd lost two front teeth, so you couldn't call it a smile. Then she took Lo's hand and suddenly seemed very anxious to get back into the house, and for me to leave. How could the day begin until I left? I'm sure she wanted the morning to race by, but who knows how a child's mind stores things, sorts through them, and works them out?

I glanced down at myself, and in a confident tone, said, "Steering may be a concern."

"Don't flatter yourself," said Lois, as if she were waiting, just waiting to say something more.

I kissed her again, lightly on the cheek, and picked up my briefcase.

I said so long to Emma again, turned, and left the porch, taking the two steps in one stride. My shoes hit the sidewalk and I cut across the lawn, kicking up dew, which tickled the hair on my bare shins above my black and grey argyles. Once in the car, I looked back at my two partners in life, framed in the doorway of our home, and with that portrait hung on the inside wall of my forehead, I waved and set off into the morning, feeling confident that the day would come out right.

I had executed just a few corners, just left our neighbourhood, when I pulled over onto the shoulder of the street, brought the car to a complete stop, and adjusted the steering wheel to a less vertical position. I was unsure if I would mention this detail to Lois; however, the thought did start me thinking about us, and not just me.

I had felt in my heart—and Lo and I had discussed it at length—that we had chosen Davide Loneson University Centre, and this particular neighbourhood to live in, as much as they had chosen us. Aside from being a picturesque campus resting atop a small mountain, DLUC is renowned for progressive attitudes, from primary and very basic codes of conduct to the more important aspects of high academic and artistic standards in all course work. There is a sincere and earnest attitude toward learning and knowledge. I had made a few friends already and no real enemies (Clarence could hardly be called an enemy), and on a community level, the same could be said of our neighbourhood: progressive, open, and friendly.

I carefully maneuvred my car onto the main road leading to University Bridge, and merged easily into the tail-end of the morning rush hour.

I had been selected by the hiring committee of the internationally renowned Department of Anthropology: Western Hemisphere. My specialization was primitive west coast art, beginning with the Moche of South America, then north on a gradual ascension through time, exploring and attempting to understand the civilizations of the Incas, Olmec, Mayan, and Aztecs primarily through their art, completing our journey with the Haida in the far-away Pacific Northwest. The course extended over both semesters, and we had not yet left what is today known as Peru. For this first exam, I would stand on the small stage at the front of the lecture hall and point out features in each pair of slides, and the students would then write short interpretive essays of contrast and comparison, cause and effect. I was most interested in the cause and effect aspect: their powers of analysis. The students had been very responsive throughout the first two months. There was no reason to doubt myself.

On this side of the bridge, as four lanes merge into two, there is always a bottleneck and I soon found myself stationary next to the bus lane. I glanced up to the row of groggy faces on my left, and they all stared straight ahead, all save one middle-aged man with a neatly trimmed hedge of grey hair that ringed his head from temple to temple. He seemed to be in a trance, looking down upon me in all my open vulnerability in my modest little car. For the briefest of moments, I thought it was my father, but of course that was impossible. I recalled the poet, a colleague in the Department of English up at DLUC, who had travelled to China in search of his lineage, and in the billions of faces there, saw his father etched into each and every countenance.

I opened my briefcase, which I had set on the passenger seat, and took out the first page of notes for the exam. I considered phoning Lo on my cellular phone, but I never liked the devices, no matter where they're installed. Besides, I didn't want to interrupt Lo's day. I knew by that time Emma would be off at kindergarten and Lo would be at work downstairs in the Loom Room weaving something beautiful. Maybe I'd call her from my office.

The vehicles around me began to inch forward, and I tried to relax. It seemed the more I tried the harder it became. The bus pulled away with its late commuters, the man who for just an instant had reminded me of my father craning his neck for as long as he could. I put the page of notes back in my briefcase and returned both hands to the wheel. Once on the bridge the traffic began moving smoothly.

As soon as I arrived in my office, I decided, I'd make a few calls. I'd call Bernie in biology (maybe he could give me something quick), or Doris, whose office was just down the hall from mine, and who specialized in Shamanism, both ancient and modern.

I adjusted my sitting position, but I still felt awkward behind the wheel. It's more that I'm a private person and would rather not stand out, or draw undue attention. I do embarrass easily. If I could conceive of a back way, a less-travelled route to my office, I'd take it, but the anthropology department offices are in the new annex to the classroom complex and there are only two ways to enter: one is through the courtyard of the Academic Quadrangle, the second, through the Admissions building. Both are heavily populated. The fire escapes are inaccessible from outside.

As I turned onto Davide Way and began my ascent, I decided to take a chance on the visitors' parking lot, which is right next to Admissions. I rolled down my window and fresh air rushed across my skin, ticklish in places, but it didn't relax me as I had hoped. It was a warm Indian summer morning, the rush hour over, and the traffic up to the

I CAN FIX ANYTHING

university very light. The leaves of the big sprawling oaks and chestnuts that lined the wide street and ran down the centre of the boulevard turned their gold undersides up in anticipation, and acorns and chestnuts lay everywhere in the shaded damp grass. Only a few clouds scattered themselves about in the sky. It did not feel like rain to me.

It was minutes past ten as I pulled into the visitors' lot and began to search for a spot, circling the long rows of cars. My class wasn't until eleven-thirty, but nonetheless, I felt pressed for time, as if I were about to find that everybody had reset their clocks without my knowledge. I had the strong sense that if I added two plus two, my sum would be odd. It was obvious I wasn't thinking clearly, and it was this sensation that made me feel that if I expected the worst, then that is how my immediate future would unfold, and, on the other side of the coin, if I hoped for the best and believed things would work out that way, then I should, likewise, expect and not be surprised by the worst. There was no winning with this flip, which contradicted my fundamental outlook on life, that being optimistic. I began to doubt on a deeper level. What reason, ever, had I for believing things should, or would, work out for the best?

There were no vacancies as I wheeled slowly around the parking lot. Had I made the wrong decision? I considered driving back down the mountain to the lower lot and boarding the shuttle. Perhaps the decrease in altitude would lower my anxiety, would calm me. I could drive fast and make the drop in elevation more sudden, except that I wasn't at all confident about speeding, and there were pedestrians and small animals to consider.

Just ahead of me, in the right lane of parked cars, I saw an import about to back out from its spot. I came to a sudden stop, and a horn sounded from behind. The little car backed out; I released the clutch and darted into the parking space. I shut off the engine, applied the hand brake, and sat for a quiet moment.

Poor Emma, I thought.

I sat for a moment longer, attempting to convince myself that my erection was small and trivial. I could deal with it or I could live with it. Either way, the world certainly wasn't going to alter itself just for me. As my mother used to say when a problem arose, you can get over it, or you can get under it. I got out of my car, grabbed my briefcase and headed towards the AQ. It was the most direct way to the anthropology department.

At ten-thirty I arrived at my office. I picked up the phone and dialed the lab.

"Bernie," I said into the receiver. "It's Sam. I need a favour."

"It sounds serious." Bernie is a small man with a slow manner, but he catches on quick. It did not surprise me that he heard the panic in my voice. He speaks across the room when he's on the phone—his distrust of telephones goes even deeper than mine—but as distant as he sounds much of the time, I've grown to like and trust him very much.

I told him I'd come right over, and then headed from my office.

Bernie didn't want to give me anything to ingest.

"Listen," I pleaded, "I'm giving an exam in less than an hour." I was looking at the top of his head, a perfectly round, shining dome of hairless skin, nodding with unintentional self-mimicry. He stood in front of me wearing sandals, his salad-bowl belly poking through his white lab coat, and he stared down at me, looking for clues, I guess. A circle of light arced back and forth over his head. It was almost hypnotic. Then he told me it seemed more psychological than biological, which was why he wouldn't give me anything to take internally. He mumbled something regarding the recent budget cuts, the closing of the psychology department.

"I can't be the first to ever experience this," I said. "Doesn't this happened to everybody?"

Bernie glanced up. "Waking up with a hard-on?" he said. "I'd estimate a little less than half the population at one time or another." Then he gave me a brief sideways look and bowed his head again. "This is a big day for you, isn't it, Sam?"

I nodded. "I'd rather not walk between a slide projector and a huge white screen like this." I made a V with my hands over my stomach. "I can't pretend it's just another day."

Bernie raised his head again. His eyebrows rose above the thick black frames of his glasses. "Perhaps you can," he said. "I have an idea." He turned from me and disappeared into his office. I had never seen him move so quickly, and I couldn't help but feel encouraged.

When he returned, truly pleased with himself, he held a

turquoise OR gown, the ancient kind that tie up in the back.

"Aw, Bernie . . . " I began, but he'd already slung it over my head, and I stood looking down at myself. "This won't do, Bernie. I feel like a tent." Upon the utterance of this last word, a shiver raced across my shoulders and a light sweat burst over my forehead.

Bernie's smile dissolved as I turned and relieved myself of the garment. I glanced at my watch, the one Lo had given me. I told him thanks anyway, left the lab, and headed back to my office. I quickly set out across the courtyard of the AQ, but I paused a moment to gaze across the big shallow pool. The fine umbrella spray of the fountain in the centre created a series of circular ripples in the square pond. I listened to the shallow water lap against the concrete sides.

As I entered the hallway, I saw Clarence walking towards me, shirtless and wearing beige safari gear. He gasped as we approached each other in the narrow passageway, then he backed against the wall in exaggerated accommodation to let me pass.

"This is just the kind of thing that happens," he said, holding his safari hat to his bare and hairless chest.

"Write a letter," I said over my shoulder as I rushed past him. It was something Clarence had always threatened to do and it had become sort of a departmental joke, though it was my first opportunity to throw it back at him.

"Conformist," he retorted, and I listened to the quick patter of his bare feet on the linoleum of the hallway as he hurried away. Clarence is a twentieth-century anthropologist, and he lives his work.

I CAN FIX ANYTHING

I walked by my open office door without so much as a pause, and on I went to the end of the hall. The door on my right was open a crack. I knocked lightly and entered.

Doris sat at her desk leaning over an open textbook. She turned in her swivel chair. An intricate silver and onyx medallion hung from her neck on a thin leather string and rested comfortably in the golden-brown valley between her large, tanned breasts.

"Oh my," she said, and sat up straight. "Sam."

Doris is in her mid-seventies, with most of those years spent wandering the mountain-tops around Machu Picchu, the interior jungles of Belize, and most recently, the Queen Charlotte Islands off the coast of British Columbia (Haida Gwaii, as the Native peoples had taught her).

"Doris," I said, leaning against the door jam. "I need some instant help."

"I see," she said, crossing her legs and calmly meshing her fingers together. "You realize I'm only human."

"My daughter is taking her floater's test today," I said, though it wasn't what I had intended to say at all. I checked my watch. "And I'm giving my first exam in less than twenty minutes."

Doris looked into my eyes. "Emma?" she said. "That's wonderful. She adores the water. You've told me this yourself."

I nodded. I could tell she wasn't about to take me seriously enough. There were obvious implications to what she was not quite saying.

"You woke up like this? You did your meditation?"

"Yes."

"Then . . ."

"I know what you're thinking, Doris. Lo wondered the same thing this morning before we climbed out of bed."

"And . . ."

"And it's a lovely way to wake up, but it didn't do any good. Twice, it didn't do any good."

Doris' gaze rose to meet my eyes. "Well," she said, "it couldn't have done any harm." Doris has the softest eyes in the department, grey-green emeralds set into a gracefully sagging face. "Like I said, Sam, I'm only human. You want me to be magic?"

I adjusted my stance in her open doorway—the resolve with which I had left my car had all but disappeared, and my full anxiety had returned. "I thought maybe there was some . . ."

"Incantation?" Doris smiled, then chuckled at my expense. "Or perhaps some magic powder? Is that what you thought, Sam? Is that how you think life works?" It was all she could do not to break into laughter, and I could tell that as soon as I left, she would have herself a hearty laugh. "You better get going," she said. "The last thing you want to be is late."

I turned to leave Doris' office, but she stopped me. "Wait," she said.

I caught the door before it closed and turned on the threshold.

"We either sink or we swim. Except, most times it's not

that obvious which is which." She smiled and returned to her book.

I retrieved my briefcase from my office and hurried over to the annex.

My lecture hall was full by eleven-thirty and I was ready to begin. The hall lights went down and the screen behind me became a bright, square gallery of light. I stepped out from behind the lectern and, just for a moment, cast my shadow in profile. I didn't know what I had expected to happen. Something. Then something did happen: a pencil dropped from a desktop in one of the upper rows and rolled down the sloping floor with the racing pace of a marble in a roulette wheel, then it stopped. There were a few quiet whispers. Someone coughed. Then silence.

The first set of slides appeared behind me. As I stepped back out of the direct light, my shoulders sagged into their normal slope and I began the exam. The fifty minutes went by without a hitch. I completed the exam and when all my students had filed out of the hall, I returned to my office with a fine layer of moisture covering my entire body: a cool, complete sweat. I took off my watch, removed my shoes and socks and sank into my high-back chair. I stared down at my erection and it stared up at me, as if taunting or daring me.

The cool fabric of my big chair surrounded me, enveloping me like water, and at that precise moment as my head floated against the soft backrest and I felt my body submerge into reverie, I remembered something I had never before remembered: it had happened years and years ago when I was just a young boy.

I was five-and-a-half when my mother took my older brother and me to the old neighbourhood pool for swimming lessons. It was an old building with cracks in the concrete floor and ceilings that dripped. Bathing trunks were, of course, required. Before we could learn to swim we had to first prove we could float the width of the shallow end on our backs. For this we would receive a blue crest in the shape of a fish that in gold-embossed lettering had *Floater* sewn into it. Once we had our crest, we could then learn to swim. The crest for *Crawlers* was even better, though I can't remember it in any detail.

With both lungs filled to their brims and my little heart beating, I pushed off from the edge of the pool floating confidently across the surface of the water—the high, high ceiling above me, the smell of chlorine, the cool water rushing past my ears and under my body, the echoes of excited divers splashing into the deep end. The older kids: the Swimmers. I tucked my chin into my neck to look over my small chest, just to see how the rest of me was doing, when I suddenly felt something was not right. My feet went first, then my legs disappeared, and my hips were following as I felt myself silently slip beneath the surface. How could this be happening? I kicked my feet and flayed my arms for just a few short moments before something even stranger happened. Just as my body was about to totally vanish, a hand reached down through my line of sight, and a huge, sturdy forefinger hooked itself onto the elastic waist-band of my red trunks, and suddenly I was not floating, nor was I sinking either. The swimming instructor walked beside me the rest of the way across the shallow end of the pool, her finger raising a tent in my trunks. And from inside, my tiny erection (as much of an erection as possible for a young boy) stared up at me with its single, humiliating eye.

When I reached the distant side, I was released. I climbed the steps and sat on the concrete lip of the pool. My face was wet and my eyes were stinging. The rest of the class floated towards me like a tiny fleet of pink boats, my older brother among them, and when I wanted to be so happy and proud, all I could do was stare down at my submerged feet on the first step, and feel deeply sad and humiliated.

Afterwards, as we all lined up to receive our crests, with our parents standing all around, my turn came, and the woman with the huge fingers and a whistle on a string around her neck produced a pair of scissors. She cut my fish in half, and handed me the head. I stood in the viewing area with a damp towel over my shoulders, my whole body in a chill, staring at the little frayed piece of blue and gold cloth in the shape of a severed fish head that I held in my hands. *Floa*, it read.

I sat in my university office atop the small mountain, overlooking the surrounding city and all its suburbs. It was at that moment that I recognized it: it was the same observant eye watching me from below, just a little older, a little more confused, and no less humbling.

EVERYTHING IS BAMBOO

There's a story I've told and retold for years and years now. Despite its familiarity, its clarity in my mind, and despite the fact that I had little else to fill my thoughts and to occupy the otherwise empty space in my cell all those years save the strange and enigmatic series of events and cast of characters composing this story, I have not been able—no, capable, not been capable—of telling this story completely, from its beginning to its end, until now. Consequently, without knowing, I had suspended myself in the middle of the story. Unless you can see the water all around, there's no way to know if it is an island or not. Being in prison is like being on an island, except that there is no losing sight of the walls.

The story (which I hesitate to call mine), I understand

I CAN FIX ANYTHING

now, begins with a letter I received at my home in Zurich just last week, and ends here, now, on this empty California beach, among the stunted and displaced bamboo staggered in the grey sand between the ocean and Betty's bungalow. Betty has stayed past the summer so that she could meet me and hear the tale completely.

✪

In 1942, for more than six weeks, I existed alone in hiding, camped just behind the dunes amid two small bamboo plantations on the coast of Morocco, south of Casablanca. The jeep I had stolen in Marrakesh took me as far as the ocean, then broke down. Not that it could have removed me from the continent, as was my objective, but it was something I kept hidden as well. It was hope, and my hope had a severed fuel-line.

Bamboo was the only material I had to work with, so I took it. Without thinking about how it came to grow there, or who it might belong to, I took it and used it. The table I ate on was a miniature bamboo raft, short lengths of bamboo lashed together with bamboo-leaf twine. The bamboo lean-to beneath which I slept each night was nearly waterproof. The chair-back I leaned against while I sat in front of my fire each evening was two thick stakes of bamboo with a panel of thinner, more pliable lengths fastened between. The lid of my food cache, too, was bamboo. I had surrounded myself with bamboo, all the while naïve to the bitter foreshadowing it cast about me, as my mind unravelled beneath the desert sun. On some days I experienced moments of clarity, trapped in the heat all day in my open bamboo cage, visions of the rest of the world, a world I could not have known, and would certainly not have trusted in anything but a vision, but these days were rare and unpredictable. To the immediate south stood a fenced-in stand of bamboo. To the north, another, and between my camp and the coastal roadway, a small grazing pasture (half the area of a football pitch) bound on the road-side by a thick hedge of bamboo.

Yet, try as I did, I could not construct from all this bamboo a single, usable fuel-line for my American-made jeep.

On this particular day, in the autumn of '42, with the morning nearly gone, I was sitting in the sand, assembling two sections of bamboo into a pipe (I fashioned a new pipe every day, as I remember, as a morning routine), and I was thinking the things I always thought about in those days, with the Atlantic waves drumming from beyond the dunes my taunting chorus. I had made it right to the edge, and there I was mired. The rest of the world went on, but I had stopped. The war, I supposed, went on too, though my escape from it had been arrested. I thought of ways to get out of Africa.

Every few days, two Moroccan children (the boy I guessed to be ten and his sister eight) herded their small flock of sheep into the pasture to graze for the afternoon. I imagined there were many such pastures along the coast, with many such flocks. The children attended closely to their shepherding duties and seemed very respectful of my camp. However, on each visit their sheep grazed nearer and nearer to my lean-to,

I CAN FIX ANYTHING

more out of curiosity than a search for greener grass. I understood that (there was no grass less yellow than any other), so I didn't think twice. Besides, I was curious too. On the most recent occasions we had even tried to converse. My French in those days was just a few phrases and some song lyrics I'd learned in Paris—only slightly better than my English—and so we mimed more than we spoke.

I had other visitors, too; all appearing out of the blue or, as it seemed, out from the bamboo. I would look up, perhaps unconsciously catching a mild scent on the breeze, and there at the crest of the nearest dune, the fisherman from the little village a mile and a half up the coast, trudged barefoot through the sand, his forefinger hooked in the gill of a three-pound bluefish; or I'd hear a clink of tin and turn to see the teenage Moroccan who sold me canned goods and army rations he had purchased from German soldiers on the black market. He had penetrating dark eyes and clay-brown skin. He spoke twelve languages, and told me he had visited cousins in Toronto, London, and even Berlin, before the war. I'd see him crossing the pasture, making his way in from the road. Sometimes he had a kind of bratwurst in a can. Sometimes he had others items as well. I called him Tin Man.

From these visitors and other merchants, I tried to learn of transport; perhaps a ship leaving Agadir bound for Buenos Aires or Caracas. Somewhere away from the war. I still believed in different continents then, different oceans. But I had received no leads, and I was constantly looking over my shoulder.

EVERYTHING IS BAMBOO

I had no way to know if anyone would come on this October day or not—my visitors' systems were not predictable, and very mysterious. I never heard, nor did I see, anyone approach from the distance. One moment the field was empty and silent, then I'd hear a squeak of laughter or a pleaful 'bahh'; I'd turn around (I remember always facing towards the ocean even though I couldn't see it for the sand dunes), and the pasture would suddenly be alive with sheep. It happened the same way with the fisherman and Tin Man. I'd be sitting there, most likely making something out of bamboo, and all of a sudden I'd look up. I could see no houses from my camp, no signs of any inhabitants in the immediate vicinity. It was eerie the first few times, but I reluctantly grew accustomed to it. On some days, I even found myself hopeful.

I heard nothing at all that day, save the call of the waves, but I turned around in the sand where I sat, half-expecting and half-hoping. . . . But it was a new visitor—I felt it even before I laid eyes on him—a visitor I'd not seen before.

A wiry old Arab sat perfectly still, erect in the swayed back of a tired and ancient grey mule, as if set there by the great hand of Allah himself. The Atlantic breeze suddenly ceased. The air was quiet throughout my camp. The big charcoal head of the beast bowed and gravity pulled its nose into the sparse grass where the meadow gave way to sand.

The face of the Arab had fixed itself upon the pile of eight-foot lengths of bamboo lying alongside my lean-to. He wore a burgundy fez, dusty and battered. When he finally turned his eyes upon me, I instinctively set down my knife and stood up in the sand. I didn't know what would happen next, but I suddenly felt guilty before this man and his mule. Although I did not know what crime I had committed, my guilt seemed obvious, even to me.

His face was small and hard: a tight, bearded knot. When his eyes narrowed a new ridge of muscle formed instantly, like a length of rope along his brow. He leaned forward on his mule, then dismounted. He took two quick steps toward my neatly stacked bamboo, raised his arm and lashed at the pile with the long switch he carried in his right hand. Its tip disappeared in mid-air, and snapped at the bamboo like an invisible snake. He turned to me. Another two steps—he could only hold his anger for so long—then his face seemed to burst wide open, unleashing a high-pitched, rabid assault, not a single word of which I could understand; yet his message, by that point, was clear.

I stepped back, tripping over my half-constructed shade, and nearly tumbled head-long into the sand. I motioned with my arms. "I no understand," I said. "*Je ne comprend pas.*" But he was not speaking French. He kicked at my bamboo chair-back and stormed about my camp. As hot as the sun beat down that day, I felt the heat of his anger press against my face with a furnace all its own.

He overturned my table with a flick from one of his wiry feet, sending the few tin plates and the set of cups into the sand. He waved his switch towards the stand of bamboo to the south, and looked me in the eye again.

Suddenly he became silent. He took the switch into his left

EVERYTHING IS BAMBOO

hand, made a fist of his right, and slammed it resolutely against his small, solid chest.

We stood for just an instant longer, the old Arab and me, facing each other in the centre of my bamboo camp. His bamboo, my camp. I had to do something.

"No," I said, my arms drifting away from my sides. "You no understand. I *found* this bamboo." I moved slowly away from him, but did not turn my back. I scrambled in the loose sand, kicking a track part way up the first dune, and I picked up a twisted grey piece of driftwood. "On the beach," I said, dropping the hunk of old wood. Then I jogged back down, through my camp right past him, and motioned to the empty pasture. "And in the field. And along the road. Dans la rue?"

He studied me with curiosity for just a moment, his face still a tight and muscled brown knot, the ridges and pathways around his eyes like a knuckled joint in a stalk of bamboo. Behind him, beyond the pasture, the distant peaks of the Atlas mountains marched silently in perfect unison inland from the sea. The Arab moved his lower jaw from side to side as if his chin were on its own unique hinge. In the quiet I heard his teeth grind.

Then I had another idea, a better idea, better than attempting to convince him of the truth, using a lie. Under my breath, but loud enough for him to hear, I said, "I'll make you a deal. I'm about to propose a trade." I made a motion with my hands as if I pulled two ends of a rope forward and back again in front of me. Not immediately, but very soon after, I believe we understood each other.

I CAN FIX ANYTHING

I pointed to the small cluster of bramble bush and branches at the north end of the pasture, opposite his plantation. "Come," I said, motioning with my hands for him to follow. I backed slowly away from my camp, watching his hands. "Come." I patted his mule as I passed it, but I kept my eyes on the old man.

He glanced at my knife in the sand near the fire pit where I had been working. He ran his tongue across his lips, then came forward slowly towards me, a wary look on his hard face, perhaps a less-guarded kind of curiosity in his small brown eyes.

He was still a few paces behind me when I arrived and began pulling the loose bushes and scrub brush away from my jeep. I had spent the entire first week trying to assemble a new line from what the environment yielded; however, bamboo is hollow only in sections. The sections are all connected in a line, but you can't necessarily get from one to the next. This proved to be my undoing.

Standing in front of my jeep, I then made the same gesture with my fist against my chest as he had made to indicate his property, his bamboo. I opened both hands and extended to him an offering. "My jeep," I said. "It's yours."

He glanced over his shoulder and called out something that sounded like "Moddi," then a sudden, short hiss shot from between his front teeth. "Psssst!"

I circled, pulling the remaining dead foliage away until the Willys was entirely exposed. It had a quarter tank of gas, I pointed out. I opened the hood and showed him the severed line, and he looked up. He nodded, and when he made a second hiss over his shoulder, Moddi raised her head and slowly ambled toward us. The old man went round to the driver's side, leaned in, and put the transmission into neutral with the familiarity of an American.

I backed away a few steps. Even though it appeared we had struck an amicable deal, I still feared for my immediate safety. He did not know me. He did not care who I was, nor where I had come from. What was I to him but a thief? Even then, while I still entertained a hope for escape, I remember suffering with the feeling that I would never get away. The world was not big enough and there was not enough time. I would be stranded forever with just this time. It was a strange, dizzying feeling that to this day weakens my knees. I was not at all sure of what was real. I kept an eye on his switch.

Moddi stood in front of the jeep, facing the road and the mountains beyond. I glanced back towards my camp and caught the glint of my knife in the noon sun. It winked of conspiracy, then of caution and fear.

He took the coiled length of rope from around Moddi's neck, fastened one end to the front bumper, and re-tied the other around the mule's neck, low so it wouldn't choke her. Then he flicked one of his quick little hands, and jumped round to the rear of his jeep. He hissed again, this time at me.

With Moddi pulling, and the old Arab and me pushing, we slowly negotiated the hard, uneven mat of the pasture. The coastal road was not paved, but it had baked into a flat, slate shelf beneath the long sun of summer, and once the jeep was in motion, Moddi was able to maintain the momentum. Her master sat behind the wheel.

What little hope I had managed to keep camouflaged, hidden, and potentially alive—I paused in the middle of the pasture and glanced back toward the road—was now heading north along the coastal highway, pulled by a mule.

Despite what the authorities claimed and later 'proved' in court, that was the first and last time I ever encountered the old Arab, one Maati Akbhar Hassan.

When I reached my camp, it was well past noon, so I crawled onto my bed-roll and pulled back the corner of the ground sheet. I took out the chunk of blond hashish I had bought from Tin Man a couple of weeks before. I located my new pipe and filled the bowl with a piece of hash the size of a pfennig. I smoked the entire pipeful.

The afternoon breeze that floated in each and every day from the Atlantic stirred the fine sand at the top of the dunes. From time to time several of the severed bamboo leaves scattered about my camp leapt suddenly back to life and jostled each other recklessly across the ground, then fell into stillness again. In the distance around me, the crackling sound of bamboo rattled on the rise and fall of this Atlantic breeze. I lay myself down, my hands folded over my sternum. Just for a few elastic moments I gazed into the sheltering blue sky, then I fell head-first into sleep.

I awoke with a start, the sun low in the western sky. I was still in a fog, yet the piercing, musty smell of sheep filled my nostrils, and seemed ready to combust my sinuses. Suddenly, there were sheep everywhere. They had surrounded and infiltrated my camp. They poked their gawky noses into my food cache, and nibbled wherever a piece of twine dangled from a bamboo joint. An old grey ewe lapped at my toes as if they were cubes of salt, and I instantly recoiled.

I scrambled from beneath my lean-to, and the sheep—there were at least two dozen—jumped a few steps, but did not follow one another back to the pasture. They stared at me, and scattered when I advanced, but they did not leave. They seemed under some spell and unable to leave.

My table was falling apart at the seams. My unfinished sun screen regressed before my eyes, collapsing back into stalks in the sand. All my work crumbled beneath their hooves. Everything I'd built fell to pieces in the sand. I waved my arms and scrambled about, but the sheep merely moved a quick couple of steps on their bony black legs, circled boldly, and then continued to graze throughout my camp.

But where were their shepherds?

It was then I noticed a long thin shadow move in from behind me, creeping up on my right. I glanced to my left—my knife was gone. I turned quickly towards the sea, and a short figure, round-headed and skinny, stood silhouetted at the top of the dune. With the orange sky behind her, the breeze made tiny wings of her cotton skirt. It was Elise, the young shepherd girl. *Mais, ou-est Pierre?*

"*Monsieur. Monsieur,*" she called, beckoning with a sweep of her arm. "*Regardez. Ici.*" She then pointed into the swale on the other side of the sand dune.

I CAN FIX ANYTHING

I tried to race up the hill, but running in sand is like running through a dream. Elise came down a few steps, reached out and took my hand. We crested the rise together.

Below, in the narrow valley between the two dunes where the sun had already set, two figures hunched over a huge, swollen ewe. Who was this stranger who had appeared from nowhere? The head of the ewe lay in the sand—her right eye wide open, reflecting a tiny bowl of moonlight through the dusk. Grains of sand clung to her nose. Her mouth opened, then opened a little wider. She was panting; breathing was difficult. Pierre stroked her neck, gently, just as he had been instructed by the man next to him.

The man with Pierre had short, cleanly cut hair and a neatly shaved neck. He looked to be about the same height and build as me. He wore a white shirt with the sleeves rolled to his biceps, and a black cummerbund around his waist. The cuffs of his black trousers were rolled up tightly around his calves and his feet were bare, as if he had been out strolling along the tideline after some formal dinner party. I had no way of knowing who it was at this point. To his left I saw a white dinner jacket folded on the sand, black shoes and socks. He leaned forward, extended his hands towards the ewe.

Above, the moon was on the rise, and the sky bristled with stars. Elise's tiny hand tightened across my palm, and I felt its warmth. Below, Mr. Bogart guided a glistening little lamb out, pink and red and slippery. The boy slipped my knife from beneath his afghan, and cut the umbilical cord a few inches from the lamb's slick belly. Mr. Bogart spoke in French to Pierre in a voice that was slow and deliberate, but I was unable to understand.

I looked down at the boy's sister, whose little hand I still held in mine, and she smiled up at me, her teeth big and white. She held up two fingers. "*Deux, Monsieur,*" she said with excitement.

Mr. Bogart leaned forward again, and his arms sank gently into the womb of the old ewe. Another lamb slid out in his cradled hands. He lay it down next to its twin. Pierre severed the second umbilical cord. My hand was suddenly empty as Elise leapt down the hill and landed in the sand next to her brother. The boy took both lambs by the hind legs, one in each hand, and held them up to me. "*Quelle bonne chance, Monsieur. Oui?*"

The ocean breeze was suddenly cold against my pupils, and I realized my eyes were wet. I nodded and raised a limp hand to young Pierre, his face gleaming with the good fortune before him.

The ewe was still for a moment while Mr. Bogart knelt beside her, running a hand along her neck and over her side. Her slackened belly rose and fell beneath his open palm. When he stood up, she too gained her footing in the loose sand. The boy set the little lambs down again, and the new mother began licking the after-birth and nibbling at the nubs of the dark cords.

Mr. Bogart unwrapped his cummerbund and wiped his hands. He picked up his shoes and jacket, then turned and came towards me up the dune, pedalling through the sand. He held out his hand and introduced himself. His hand was sticky.

"I'd wager you could use a drink, pal," he said in the same deliberate tone, though this time he spoke in German, not French or English.

"Yes," I said. "A drink." (I find it impossible, even now, to believe he was in Morocco starring in a motion picture, and I had to confess that I was unfamiliar with his work in Hollywood.)

He took a cigarette from his shirt pocket, flicked his thumbnail across a match-head, and lit the smoke.

We descended into my camp, and I searched out the two largest of the tin cups that had been knocked into the sand by the sheep while Mr. Bogart gathered up bamboo splinters and lit a fire.

I held out the cups and he poured brandy from a flask he kept in the breast pocket of his coat, and we drank to the newborns. He offered me a cigarette; our smoke floated over the fire and was lifted silently into the huge sky above us.

Mr. Bogart glanced around and I followed his eyes. The sheep waited, hovering on the outskirts of my demolished camp. Their sporadic nasal pleas, haunting in the semi-darkness, called for their shepherds to take them away.

Mr. Bogart had paused on his coastal journey southward in a small village to the north of my camp, and there he heard an old Arab boasting in a café about how his performance as a plantation owner had netted him a jeep. The unsuspecting foreigner was still camped on the beach.

"He also told me," said Mr. Bogart, "that you were an American." Cigarette smoke slipped from his mouth.

"I honestly didn't believe I was stealing from anybody," I told him. The last sip of brandy lit a path down my throat, and I held out my cup for more. "You must know that."

"Of course," he said, reaching with the flask around the small fire. "Who could have known? Bamboo always grows in straight lines behind fences. Strange beast, that bamboo." He smirked sarcastically. "You know what else?" He gazed across our fire, shadows leaping about his face. "You, I believe, are a doomed man."

I did not, at the time, know why he should say such a thing, but suddenly I felt the same dizzying sense of guilt and hopelessness I had felt before the old Arab. I was out of my element. I was not in control.

The two young shepherds came over the dune, a lamb in each one's arms, the ewe scrambling behind. A sheep's hooves are not designed for deep and sandy terrain. The flock followed their shepherds out to the pasture, and they all soon disappeared into the twilight.

I turned back to Mr. Bogart. "But whose bamboo was it, then?" A pleading tone crept into my voice, which I feebly tried to mask. "Won't he go to the authorities?"

"He can't go to the authorities." Mr. Bogart drained his cup, and his face hovered above the fire like a demon.

I asked him to help me, to harbour me, and to aid in my

escape from the continent. He told me about Hollywood, the Pacific Ocean, and the beaches of California. He told me about the woman he had met recently, while shooting this film. She was young, only half his age, but he was sure to marry her.

"You understand," he said, with what now seems a wry tone, "I thought you were American." He tossed his cigarette butt into the fire. "I've already helped you, I'm afraid," he said, but I didn't understand then, what he meant, what he had done. Then he pointed towards the pasture beyond my camp.

He told me he had acquired the jeep from the old Arab in the village to the north. Just a few metres beyond my fallen lean-to sat my old battered jeep. He stood up then, in the sand, holding his silver flask at one side, his bundle of attire at the other. He said goodbye to me in one of his idioms (I can't remember which because it's only been reinforced by the film roles I've seen him in since). He turned, drifted up the sand, and over the first dune. I watched as he crested the second dune, then disappeared completely. How could I have not heard him drive up in my jeep? Did I sleep that deeply?

The next day the police were waiting for me at an insignificant-looking roadblock on the outskirts of Casablanca. I was taken into custody, and tried and convicted quickly for the murder of Maati Akbhar Hassan. I escaped from prison thirty-five years later, in 1977, with the help of a nurse when I contracted hepatitis and it appeared as if I might die. I travelled by fishing boat to Sicily, where I acquired papers and a passport. I laid low for several years until it was safe to access my Swiss bank account. I changed my name several times.

✪

The sun was low in the sky over Betty's beach, falling toward the distant Pacific horizon. I watched the waves lumber in repeatedly as if on some tireless and long-forgotten duty, blundering onto shore with the grace of a drunk and uninvited guest. The same ocean, really, the world over. A different name, but a part of the same salty waters.

In her letter Betty had written that she wanted to know about her husband, the famous Hollywood actor. The letter was brief and straight-forward, as was our meeting by the pool. He'd been dead all these years. She needed something more, needed to know something more, something new that she had not known before. I could understand that. We all need something new. So I told her. And she believed me. A part of her did not want to believe me, but she did. I know she did.

And I realized something as I stood there on the beach with the ocean stretching out before me—which is something that is supposed to happen at the end of a story—as my feet found their forms in the dry, late afternoon sand above the high tideline. We are only ideas in the minds of others and, what's more, we do not even count in our own realities, in our own visions of the world, only in the minds of others.

I CAN FIX ANYTHING

The waves lapped and overlapped the shore. The bamboo rattled in the breeze behind me. I tasted salt on my lips. And it was real. It was finally real.

GARY WHITEHEAD's work has been published in numerous publications, including *Canadian Fiction, Prism international, Writing,* and *Dandelion.* He is also a co-founder of the Kootenay School of Writing. He lives on Salt Spring Island, B.C.